A GLORIOUS DAY IN HELL
The Day Jesus Descended

John Eudy

"...He suffered under Pontius Pilate,
was crucified, died, and was buried.
He descended into hell.
On the third day, he rose again..."

The Apostles' Creed

Contents

Prelude: A Sudden and Terrible Realization

The sounds of battle echo down a well-traveled, middle eastern road. A loud "thunk" sound reverberates through a Roman Legionnaire's chest before he falls to the ground. Everything goes silent.

Ioannes opens his eyes. The sky is no longer blue. The dust, stirred up by battle, no longer swirls in the air around him. Instead, he sees an ethereal, almost post-twilight, sky. He looks out over a now silent battlefield, only the dead are present; they lie on the ground around him. Time has stopped. Nothing is moving. There is no sound. The sky and land have turned a gray, muted color.

He turns his gaze downward only to see his own 19-year-old body lying on the ground. Shock sets in as he stares at an arrow protruding from the seam of his body armor; his lifeless hands still clutch the pole bearing his legion's standard. Ioannes looks up and around in bewilderment, staggering backward in disbelief. Dropping his head down once again and raising his hands, he looks at his open palms. As he does, he suddenly realizes he is completely naked. He lowers his hands, instinctively covering his genitalia, and begins to look up with paranoia.

Without warning, a pair of callous hands grasp his forearms tightly from the rear and yanks them behind him. Simultaneously, a coarse, foul-smelling burlap sack is thrust over his head and pulled tight around his neck. Bits of twilight shine through the dark burlap while he begins to wrestle with his captors. Ioannes is unable to break free and soon feels metal shackles clamping shut around his wrists. He grunts as he feels the thrust of his captor's heel against the back of his knees. Forced painfully to the ground, everything becomes silent once more.

A growling, guttural voice breaks the silence, "Heh, heh, heh. Another sinner for the pit!" Higher-pitched cackling emanates from all around him now. Ioannes, unable to see any clear details through the burlap, knows deep in his gut something bad is about to happen.

Chapter 1: So Many Questions

Fierce fighting continues on an ancient middle eastern road. A Roman Centuria[1], holding their phalanx formation, repels raiders attacking from surrounding hills near the summit of a mountain pass. Near the front of the column of troops, there, in the middle of the phalanx, is a seasoned veteran named Cælius. Though he is only 27, he has seen battle before. This time is different though.

A rage stirs in his breast; an old fury that resided in the darker corners of his heart. Quietly aware of its existence for years, Cælius has always thought he might appease it as a soldier, but now rises uncontrollably to the surface. It makes his hands shake and his temperature rise. Sweat beads on his forehead run past his brow and drip from his chin. A low growl rumbles through clenched teeth. Throwing his shield and spear into the dirt, he suddenly breaks ranks and draws his gladius. His growling erupts into a blood-curdling war cry as he rushes madly toward an enemy raider.

---

[1] 80-man unit

The raider thrusts his sword at the Roman with his right hand. Cælius, in stride, steps to his right avoiding the thrust, instinctively raises his left arm, hitting his opponent's forearm, and knocking his sword hand upward. He then mercilessly runs his gladius upward into the enemy's chest. Cælius stands, holding the raider upright, impaled upon his gladius. He stares into his eyes, watching life leave his enemy. Finally, he lets go of the sword. His enemy falls to the ground; Cælius stands over the bloodied corpse breathing heavily.

The unbridled wrath departs, and he slowly regains his consciousness and his senses. Both remorse and fear overcome him. He realizes he is not only out of formation and exposed, but a foreign sense of regret permeates his mind. Looking around the dusty, rocky area, he sees the bodies of the enemy littering the ground while a handful of raiders flee back over the ridgeline. Their retreat signals the end of the battle. Cælius takes a deep breath in relief.

Feeling calmer, he looks toward the front of his Centuria and sees a banner missing. He pulls his gladius from the chest of his enemy, instinctively wipes the blood from the blade, and sheathes it. He rushes toward the banner carriers, parting other soldiers from their formation until he reaches the carriers. There he sees his friend Ioannes lying on the ground. He drops to his knees, lifts the dead soldier's body, and places his back on his raised knee. He takes the banner from his lifeless hands and hands it to a random soldier within the formation. In a sad, almost tearful voice, he says, "My brother. Why must it be you to fall this day?"

Another Legionnaire moves up through the ranks to where Cælius is. Stopping next to Cælius, he observes in a dismissive tone, "Isn't that Ioannes? Is he not the one who refuses to fight? Why do you mourn him so Cælius? His death is not a significant loss."

Cælius slowly looks up at the intrusive legionnaire. Angered and annoyed by his comment, he retorts, "We are all brothers, are we not?"

The Optio[2] approaches. Older, and much gruffer, he barks out orders while physically moving soldiers in the direction he wants them to go. "You, get back in formation! You, help

---

[2] 2nd in command of Centuria

gather our dead! You, go help dig graves over there." He points to a sandy, gravely area north of the road. He then stops and points to Cælius and the other legionnaire, commanding, "You two, strip that man of his armor and put it in the cart coming up. Afterward, take his body to the grave. Then clean up and get back in formation." Having given all his commands, he returns to his previous station.

The two soldiers obey their orders and begin stripping the armor off Ioannes' body. As they do, Cælius, who is looking down, reflects on a conversation he recently had with his slain friend.

* * * * *

It was a late day in Cæsarea Maritima. A soothing breeze was blowing in off the water. Having completed their tasks and given liberty for the evening, Cælius and Ioannes sit on part of a rock wall facing the wind and the Mare Internum[3]. Low tidal waves splash at their feet below. The occasional gull squawks in the air overhead and a bustling market can be heard in

---

[3] Mediterranean Sea – (translated from Latin)

the distant background. Neither soldier has his helmet or spear, however, for safety's sake, they still wear their armor and carry their gladius at their side.

Ioannes is looking down at the waves breaking on the sea wall below him. Cælius, sitting a couple of feet away, gazes out at the open ocean. He is always mesmerized by the deep blue sea. Today though, he has something to ask his young friend. "I've heard rumor Ioannes, that you will not fight. That you lack the courage to kill." He pauses for effect. "You march with the legion, you even carry our banner, but you do know you will never be considered a true Legionnaire unless you fight. We are rewarded in eternity for what we do in life. If you want to see the green fields of Elysium, you must overcome your fears."

Cælius looks over at Ioannes, who keeps his head down, still observing the water splashing against the wall. Cælius grows slightly indignant, "Do you hear me Ioannes? Soon we will reach Hierosolyma[4]. Beyond that, we will claim territory, treasure, and slaves in Augustus Cæsar's name. Those people will not be

---

[4] Jerusalem (translated from Latin).

submissive either. You must find the courage to fight."

Ioannes turns to his right to look at his friend and mentor. Though they are far enough away from others, he still speaks in a low tone so as not to be overheard. Somewhat nervous, he is hesitant in his response, "I do not fear Bellum[5], Cælius. I simply have no desire to take a human life; I just cannot bring myself to it. I am content in my humble service to you and other soldiers. I am happy to cook, serve meals, build roads, shore up fortifications, or whatever is needed. I am even more proud to carry the banner for the legion. I simply have no desire for violent conquest. I only seek to find the truth of God in my service and my travels."

Cælius, his chain of thought broken by Ioannes' words, turns to look at him with curiosity. "Ah, there it is again, your God. Tell me more about this god you've discovered."

Ioannes, realizing he just mentioned God inadvertently, quickly turns his attention back down to the waves below. He is reluctant to respond, but, after an awkward silence, eventually faces Cælius again. "I can only say

---

[5] war (translated from Latin)

that I believe the God of the Iudæus[6] people *is* the one true God." He pauses and takes a deep breath before continuing, "I believe he is merciful, loving, and more powerful than the gods we Romans worship. His prophets of old accomplished such miraculous things with his aid and in his name. Moreover, we have yet to even receive his son, the Messias. It is for his sake I do not kill; that I serve the legion the way I do. It is for him that I no longer indulge in the sins of the flesh."

Ioannes pauses again. He returns his attention to the waves lapping the wall below. In a soft tone, he says, "I, I have said too much. If you sincerely want to know more, and if I can trust you, my friend, we can speak again when we reach Hierosolyma."

Cælius is reflective. "Hmm." He begins. "You're a fine young man Ioannes; I'll keep your secret for now. Maybe I will even give your offer of a deeper conversation some consideration while we march tomorrow." Cælius stands. "Well, you can sit here if you like; however, it has been a long journey thus far and, unlike you, I **am** going to indulge in wine,

---

[6] Jewish (translated from Latin)

women, and food. I'll see you back at camp later tonight my friend."

Cælius collects himself and then turns to leave. He walks confidently toward the gate leading into the city from the sea wall.

Ioannes remains seated on the break wall. Thinking his friend and mentor is far enough away, he raises his eyes to the bright blue sky and prays to a God he barely knows, "Deus Meus, it is YOU I fear, and YOU I love. Grant me the strength and courage to do what is right."

Cælius hears Ioannes praying. He stops silently in his tracks for a moment and turns his head slightly to his left to listen to the prayer. When Ioannes is done, he mumbles a "harumph," turns his head back, and walks on toward the gate in the sea wall.

* * * * *

It's night now and the city celebrates. Soldiers and sailors indulge themselves in whatever pleasure is to be had. Cælius emerges from the cloth-covered doorway. He looks left and right as he adjusts his armor and gladius. Legionnaires solicit prostitutes on either side of the entrance to the lupanar[7]. Although he should be somewhat content, having slaked his lust, he has a somber look on his face. He glances up and down the alley before walking left past all the revelers. Cælius rounds a corner to his right and strolls out into the main thoroughfare. He turns left again and walks about a block before entering a tavern searching for food and drink.

He spies a small table in the back, away from the bar and other partiers. He takes a seat there with his back to the wall. As if knowing what he wants, a server brings him an empty cup, a flagon of wine, bread, and a couple of figs. He gives her two coins, and she moves on. He pours the wine into his cup, throws back the first round, and then pours another.

He leans back in his chair, placing his left hand on his thigh while keeping his right on his cup. Cælius stares past the bar and out into the lively streets. *What is this feeling?* He broods. *Why do I find no pleasure in eating, drinking, or having sex? What is this empty feeling within me?* He contemplates this while slowly eating the bread and figs and sipping his wine.

---

[7] Brothel (translated from Latin)

He sets his empty cup down on the table. Intertwining his fingers in front of his cup, and leaning his face toward his clasped hands, his firm chin hovering above his empty cup, he thinks, *I come from a hearty, seafaring family, who never questioned the gods. Why do I question them now? Why does the idea of a single, living God bring such unrest to my heart and mind?* Cælius looks down at the plate and cup in front of him. He surveys what little remains. "Maybe Ioannes will have an answer. I will speak with him when we reach Hierosolyma." He reassures himself. Unlocking his fingers, he reaches for his flagon of wine and fills his cup. He takes a bite of the remaining bread and then puts the cup to his lips. He throws his head back, gulping the entire cup of wine. He sets the cup back on the table and pours another.

* * * * *

The next day has come and the legion marches along the Via Maris[8]. The ranks move along quietly. Many legionnaires are

---

[8] Ancient road from Cæsarea to the Roman citadel in Ioppe

overcoming their previous evening's indulgences as they trudge along. Cælius is disquieted and agitated. His thoughts are plagued by thoughts of this God Ioannes speaks of. Although he doesn't understand why, he knows all the emptiness, anger, and unrest are related to his doubts and queries.

The soldier marching to his right quickly glances in Cælius' direction and sees the confounded look in his eye. "What troubles you Cælius? What irritates you so?"

"Nothing!" He barks. "It's nothing."

The soldier, slightly offended, decides to ignore the anti-social Cælius, who is happy to march on in silent contemplation.

* * * * *

Later that evening, the road-weary legion files into the Ioppe Citadel. Soldiers, tired from their march, break formation and head to various places within it. Cælius does not speak to others after entering the citadel himself. Instead, he is of a single thought: find Ioannes.

Cælius comes across him, securing his shield and spear for the night. He walks up to Ioannes, grabs his shoulder, and urges him to turn around. Turning to face his friend, Ioannes sees he is upset about something. Before he can say anything, however, Cælius says in a low, secretive tone, "I am disturbed by this notion of a single, living God who involves himself in our daily lives, Ioannes. Tomorrow, we cross the Judean mountains. Once we reach our destination, you and I must speak about this in greater detail." Cælius turns and departs hastily before Ioannes can answer. Unsure of his friend's enigmatic statement, Ioannes spends the rest of the evening in prayer.

* * * * *

That was yesterday, before the ill-fated raid. Now, random soldiers lean on shovels, wipe dirt from their faces, and drink water from their skins. Their hard work digging a mass grave has been completed. Cælius and the other legionnaire lower Ioannes' body, which has been stripped down to his tunic, into the grave. The other soldier climbs out, while Cælius remains. His uniform is covered in dust and soaked with sweat. He takes a deep breath and kneels next to Ioannes' body. He removes two small, silver coins from a purse on his belt, and gently places them on the eyes of his friend. "I hope your God has granted you entry into his Elysium my friend. If not, this will pay for your journey across the River Styx."

Cælius stands and wipes the sweat from his brow. At that very moment, an authoritative voice rings in his ears, "Cælius, you will not see my Elysium if you continue in your ways." Startled, he looks around, but no one is near enough to speak to him. His heart beats rapidly. A shiver runs down his spine, and he is unable to control the tears glazing his eyes. The voice speaks again, "It is time to seek a new path." Deep down, he knows he has heard the voice of the one true God, and nothing else will ever be the same for him.

Chapter 2: A Soldier's Descent

Ioannes kneels on an old mountain road turned into a battlefield. He sees nothing with clarity for the rancid burlap sack covering his head. He can just make out the sky, which is a strange mix of twilight and gray as if there were an evening thunderstorm, and bits of the dark tan and muted land. Shackles clink against chain behind his naked body. He sees blurs of movement as his captors circle around him.

A band of four short dæmons led by an exceptionally large fiend surrounds two humans. The larger demon points his axe toward Ioannes and another, unseen soul, and commands in a deep, snarling voice, "Chain them together and bring them along."

The little goblin-like dæmons rush about, pulling Ioannes to his feet and wrapping chains around his bare waist. The unnamed soul thrashes in resistance, pulling Ioannes backward. The Dæmon Captain unleashes his whip, cracking it against the flesh of the unnamed soul, who screams and curses as he falls, "Scum! Damn you, little freaks!" His hands are bound, and a burlap sack is pulled over his head as well. He kicks blindly at the goblin dæmons who are violently grappling him, trying to make him stand up.

Ioannes can barely make out the back of the Dæmon Captain as he straps his axe to his back. He then bends down to pick up the chain lead, shouting, "Get up and get moving! Or I will give you another stripe, you worthless sinner!" He snorts and then yanks the lead chain. Ioannes nearly loses his footing as he lurches forward. He strikes his foot on a jagged stone, slicing it. He stumbles but, not wanting to feel the sting of the whip, limps forward in pain.

Ioannes assumes the unnamed soul is one of the fallen raiders who attacked his Centuria, but he can't be sure. Quietly walking now, the slow-moving procession moves away from the battlefield on the road. Ioannes hears the shouts of dæmons capturing and chaining others around him, likely soldiers and raiders from the same skirmish.

As he trudges along, he begins to think, *I only wanted to find the truth of God. Was my lack of courage to fight and kill what led to this exile in the underworld? Or was it something worse? Did the one, true God find me unworthy and send me here? What did I do to offend him so;*

to be cast down? His thoughts turn toward his youth.

* * * * *

The late afternoon sun warms the rolling green hills. Young Ioannes, dressed in a clean, white tunic, scampers across the verdant land of the quaint hillside vineyard. The 10-year-old boy weaves and wanders around rows of grape vines, occasionally plucking a cluster here and there from the vines, and placing them in a small basket. Nibbling on one or two grapes as he walks, he tries to talk to some of the servants but is often shooed away as an annoyance. Eventually, he gives up and trots back to his villa with the basket mostly full of grapes.

Later in the evening, just after dusk, the young Ioannes sneaks out of his villa. He cradles a small, but relatively full, burlap bag, running as silently as he can toward the servant's quarters. There he stops in front of a wooden door at one of the small houses and knocks.

The door creaks open in short order and the youthful Ioannes is greeted by a gruff, elderly man, who immediately crosses his arms over his small round belly. He tucks his bearded face down to give the boy an 'unwelcome' look. The youth is clearly not intimidated, however. He peers past the older man to see his wife and two children, one a boy about 8 years old and the other a girl the same age as he is. They are reclining on cushions around a short, Middle Eastern table.

Ioannes looks back up at the frowning father who, after a final scowl, quickly opens his arms and give a large smile, greeting him with a quiet, but jovial tone, "Aw, who am I fooling? Ioannes my boy! Shalom! What are you doing out here?" The father glances outside the door, first left, and then right. "You know you're not allowed here, especially this late."

"I know, but I wanted to bring you something."

"Ah, let's get you in where it's safe. Come in, come in." The man motions for the boy to enter. Ioannes does so swiftly and takes his sack to the table where the rest of the servant family happily greets him. The father again cautiously looks both ways outside the door before closing it.

Inside, Ioannes eagerly empties a loaf of bread, three peaches, and a small wadded-up tunic from his sack onto the little table. The mother reaches over to pat him on the head and caress his cheek as only a mother can do, "Oh, thank you Ioannes. You're such a good boy!"

Taking the small tunic and the peaches with her, she gets up and goes into the tiny kitchen area. Her husband comes to the table. Exhausted from working in the vineyard, he groans as he reclines to the left of the young lad. He motions for their guest to sit. The children scooch around the table so there is room for him to sit with them.

"Well, my boy!" He begins with an exhale of breath. "Truly you are a fine young man. God bless you." The father leans across the small table toward Ioannes and motions with his finger to come a bit closer. "In our language, your name is Yohanan. It means 'God is gracious.'" The man winks at him. "Indeed, he is, yes?" He then reclines at the table again, smiles at his children, and in a more jovial tone, says, "Yes, I think that's what we will call you from now on; Yohanan." His children smile in agreement.

Young Ioannes smiles too with an affirmed delight. The mother, who has put the fruit away for later, returns to the table with tea. She sets one more cup out for their guest and pours everyone a small amount. The father takes his cup in hand, lifts it to his nose, and breaths deep of its aroma. He exhales, "Ahhhh. Smells delicious mother." He then happily sips his hot tea.

Ioannes, in his youthful impatience, unexpectedly blurts out, "I would like to know more about your God. Would you be willing to teach me?"

The father sputters, nearly choking on his tea at the question. His children giggle at the sight of their father being caught off guard. He sets his cup down, brushes off tea from his beard, and raises his eyebrows in slight surprise. He clears his throat and says, "Hmmm... well now, that is a large, and sudden, request. What would your parents think if they knew I taught you such things?"

Ioannes shrugs his shoulders and looks inquisitively at the father, who, in turn, glances at the mother. She nods reassuringly, "Go on papa. Surely Adonai will smile on you for teaching the boy."

He turns back to face the young man and lets out a short sigh. "Well then Yohanan, I suppose we could teach you a little bit. How about his commandments? Yes, let's start there." The father begins to warmly and patiently instruct young Ioannes and his own children. "The first commandment is to worship Adonai alone. We are never to worship any other false gods or idols. He is a jealous God who desires the attention and affection of his children..."

* * * * *

Time passes. Twilight gives way to the darkness of night and Ioannes' mother becomes aware of his absence. She flings open the door of their villa. She is upset and is frantically looking for her son. He is not to be found in the house, so she races to the stables. He is not there either. She stops to think for a minute. Remembering his growing fondness for the servants, she rushes to their quarters.

She does not knock, instead, she simply barges into each house, one by one until she finally bursts into the Iudæus[9] family's home. A startled Ioannes whips around to see his angry mother glaring at him. Driven by both fear and anger, his mother scolds him. "There you are. What are you doing out at night and in here no less?! Come with me! Now!" Ioannes's Mother storms over to the table and grabs him by the wrist. She pulls him to his feet, and then drags him out of the quarters. Ioannes looks back to the father who lovingly smiles while shrugging. The young man waves back to him before disappearing around the corner.

* * * * *

Ioannes, the man, ponders this memory as he stumbles down this new, unseen path into the underworld, *What the Iudæus servants believed always struck me as true. It was they who led me to believe a living God who loved and cared for them was better than any Roman god. The Roman gods seemed to want to use humanity for their selfish whims and desires.*

He remembers making many secret visits to his favorite Iudæus family over the years. They

---

[9] Jewish (translated from Latin).

taught him about the prophets of old and of a coming Messias; one who would save his people from slavery, tyranny, and oppression in this world and the afterlife. He was drawn to the Messias and he thinks, *Although I never became fully Jewish, I wondered if he would save me too.*

* * * * *

Years later, a teenage Ioannes, now 16 years old, is seated at the dinner table, eating supper with his family. Ever the brash young man, he talks about his conversations with the servants. He tries to express his understanding of the Ten Commandments and the Messias as it was taught to him.

The discussion is a visibly uncomfortable one for his parents and siblings. His brother and sister eat quietly with their head down. Their father has a look of distant concern on his face. Ioannes, in his naivety, speaks in a semi-joyful voice, uninhibited but still respectful, "...I think the commandments are just and I'm fascinated by their Messias."

Ioannes' father interrupts with a dismissive voice, "Give no credence to such lies son; you should ignore the servants and their nonsense! There is more than one god and you need to start paying attention to them, or else you will find yourself cursed." The room falls silent. Everyone, including the dejected Ioannes, eats the rest of their meal quietly.

* * * * *

Ioannes feels the tug of the chains and hears his captors goad him along. He thinks back to how he came to serve in the legion. He recalls his parents' disapproval of the Iudæus' beliefs, his subsequent rejection of the Roman gods, and his quiet internalization of the one true God's commandments. He remembers the hunger for the deeper truth, which had been cultivated within his heart. As Ioannes grew older, he also grew tired of his father's chastisement and squabbling with his family over his persistent belief in Elohim.

Once he entered manhood, he decided to leave home and serve in the Roman Legion. This would allow him to expand his knowledge of God and find the truth. So, at the age of 18, Ioannes joined the legion and left his home.

Thinking it divine providence, he was overjoyed to find out he was to be assigned to a garrison headed for Hierosolyma itself.

He quickly learned to guard his faith, however; to never openly profess to be a follower of Elohim as a Roman soldier. Though he hoped privately following God's commandments might still grant him entry into Elysium one day. He dreamed of walking near the living God under the blue sky of his Elysian Fields; feeling the eternal light upon his face. *Instead, I find myself here.* He thinks to himself.

The procession moves along an ancient, wide, and well-worn, stone road leading downward into a desert-like valley and ending at a cave entrance on a barren mountainside. Though he cannot see it, the valley itself resembles a gaping wound in the land; like once fertile earth had been slashed open by evil. Darkness permeates the foul-smelling burlap sack over Ioannes' head. Occasional glimpses through tiny holes show the surrounding environment grows more barren. The vegetation has dwindled. There are no trees, no grass, only an occasional dried-up shrub or sickly-looking weed springs up between rugged rocks. The once star-laden sky has vanished too. Now, just an ever-darkening atmosphere blankets the procession as it makes its way toward the cave. All is silent, save for the shuffling of feet on the ground, the prisoner's chains rattling, and the goblin dæmon's raspy, high-pitched gossiping.

"These humans just don't comprehend it do they? Romans, Arabs, Jews, Africans, they all fall. They're all ours." States the first dæmon.

One of them giggles, and then pokes Ioannes in the left shoulder with something sharp, "You hear that, **boy**? No Elysium for you. Hee, hee, hee!"

Ioannes says nothing, he just keeps plodding forward. They enter the yawning maw of the mountain cave. Moist, stale air greets them. A massive rust-covered gate lay about 300 feet into the cavern. Moss and lichen-covered parapets of black and gray stone rise at each side of the gate. Water drips from rows of stalactites onto stalagmites which run from the parapets to the cavern walls on each side. From a distance, the scene resembles a monstrous, salivating mouth. Fire pits glow orange-yellow from behind the rock 'teeth', illuminating the scene and casting shadows all around.

The procession slows as it approaches the gate. With a deep, commanding growl, the Dæmon Captain, calls them to a halt, "Stooooop! Fools." He loudly drops the chain lead on the ground and walks toward his captives. Sandaled footsteps fall heavily on the stone path as he slowly circles the unnamed soul behind Ioannes. "Shall I tell you what the sign over your head reads?"

The unnamed soul pulls defiantly at his chains and curses, "I don't give a damn what it says, filthy creature!"

"Filthy!?" He responds and rushes upon the shade of a man, punching him in the head. The unnamed soul immediately falls to the ground, the weight of his fall pulling Ioannes backward. The Dæmon Captain, who moves with inhuman speed to Ioannes' side, growls in Ioannes' ear, "What about you, wretch?"

Heavy though it is, the burlap sack over his head ripples with each exhale of the Dæmon Captain's putrid breath. He does not respond; Ioannes simply lowers his head, waiting to be assaulted. Dæmon Captain backs slightly away, and then snarling, begins circling his captives again.

The goblin-like dæmons pick the unnamed soul up off the ground, standing him back up. Dæmon Captain says in a slow, haughty cadence, "No guesses? Fine! I will gladly tell you what it says, so you understand your situation. Though you cannot see them, we are at the Devorandum[10] Gate of hell itself. The beautiful sign over your head reads, 'Abandon all hope ye who enter here'." He stops in front of the procession, raises his arms, and says in a triumphant tone, "Welcome to eternal damnation you pathetic fools! Ha, ha, ha!"

The clanking sound of iron and the high-pitched grind of rusty metal is heard as the gates open wide in the dank cavern. Dæmons manning the gate, as well as the dæmon escort, break out in cheers and maniacal laughter.

Dæmon Captain spits at the feet of his captives before bending down to pick up his lead again. With a yank of the chain and demonic laughter, the procession continues its descent through the Devorandum Gate and into hell.

---

[10] Devour, swallow, or gulp down (translated from Latin)

Chapter 3: Crossing the River Styx

The hell-bound procession has walked for some time. The scenery, if you could call it that, has changed. The road has narrowed and now winds toward a riverbank of jagged pumice, obsidian boulders, and a black sand shore. Sounds of wailing, screaming, and cursing are heard in the distance. The road draws closer to the dark, mud-colored water of the River Styx, which flows and glistens in the dim light.

A wooden ship, similar to a Roman hemiolia, has run up on the bank in the distance. It has a narrow draft and only one row of oars on each side. A makeshift gangway of hastily cut, wooden planks, extends from its deck just behind the bow to the gravel beach. Wailing and the sounds of whips cracking on flesh grow louder and louder as the procession nears.

Several goblin-like dæmons herd shades up the gangplank, whipping and beating them as they board. As Ioannes' procession draws near, Charon, the ship's captain and ferryman on the River Styx, arrogantly approaches the railing. He is a gaunt, older man with a long, unkempt white beard. Wiry arms protrude from his dirty tan tunic and a small gray cloak hangs over his shoulder. He glares down over the railing at the Dæmon Captain and his captives. He offers an indignant greeting, "More for darkness and fire, I presume?"

Dæmon Captain snorts at his derision, "Of course! You will allow us to escort them, yes?"

"Hrmph. Throw them in the hold and come aboard." Charon mumbles under his breath, "Scurvy bilge rat, that one."

The Dæmon Captain reluctantly nods with false gratitude and then yanks the chain forward toward the gangway. Ioannes, still hooded, feels the wood under foot, but before he can navigate his way, he is shoved from behind by one of the dæmons and stumbles up the gangplank.

Not able to see when he is at the top, he steps off the gangplank and falls on the hard, wooden deck, hurting his shoulder and head. Surrounding dæmons laugh gleefully before quickly seizing him, and the one chained behind him. They shove them both toward the boat's hold.

Below decks is a burly creature, whose features are difficult to make out in the shadowy hold. His massive, clawed hands reach for the two souls and forcefully pull them down inside the hold. There he shoves them to the side of the hull to make room for more. It isn't long before the ship is packed full of captured souls. The burly dæmon exits the hold and loudly slams the wooden hatch closed.

The ship's hold is completely dark, Ioannes can see nothing but blackness. Moments later, he hears the oars scaping the hull as they are extended outboard. Some plunk into the water and some land on the gravelly shore. They scratch and splash pulling the soul-laden boat out into open water.

Charon's raspy voice rings out, "Row damn you! Row!" A whip cracks and the sound of the boat's keel scraping the rock on its way back out into the River Styx echoes briefly in the hold.

Above decks, wingless, seagoing dæmons skulk about. Dæmon Captain leans against the main mast and looks out over the muddy river. He growls at any crewman or other dæmon brave, or naïve, enough to come too close.

Hoping to both instill despair into his cargo and get his scurvy crew working in rhythm, Charon sings a sea shanty (a variation of "Leave Her Johnny, Leave Her"). Holding fast to the

rudder, he guides the ship to its destination
while singing in a loud, gruff voice,
   "The winds blew foul, and the seas ran high.
   Leave her sinner, leave her.
   We shipped up green and none went by
   And it's time for us to leave her,
   Leave her sinner, leave her,
   Oh, leave her sinner, leave her,
   Oh, the voyage is done and the winds don't
blow
   And it's time for us to leave her."
   The dæmon crew joins in while handling lines,
rowing, or working on other tasks. Their low
tones make the shanty sound more like a dirge
as the ship slowly plies the muddy waters.
   "The old man swears, and the mate swears
too,
   Leave her sinner, leave her.
   The crew all swear, and so would you
   And it's time for us to leave her,
   Leave her sinner, leave her,
   Oh, leave her sinner, leave her.
   Oh, the voyage is done and the winds don't
blow
   And it's time for us to leave her.
   The rats have gone and we the crew

Leave her sinner, leave her.
It's the time be-damned that we went too
And it's time for us to leave her,
Leave her sinner, leave her,
Oh, leave her sinner, leave her.
Oh, the voyage is done and the winds don't blow
And it's time for us to leave her.
Well I pray that we shall ne're more see
Leave her sinner, leave her.
A hungry ship, the likes of she
And it's time for us to leave her,
Leave her sinner, leave her,
Oh, leave her sinner, leave her.
Oh, the voyage is done and the winds don't blow
And it's time for us to leave her."

The crew's song soon ends, and, except for the hull creaking, rhythmic oaring, and occasional shade moaning, all is quiet. Ioannes peers through a small hole in his sackcloth hood. He cannot see anything in the darkness but can hear muffled weeping. *Oh, my head and shoulders.* He thinks. *Is that water or blood on my feet?* He wonders if this was how prisoners and slaves are treated after the Roman army captured them. He knows those who taught him about Adonai were slaves, *did they suffer in this way?* He thinks to himself. An intense sadness for them overcomes him, which in and of itself becomes an unexpected burden on his soul.

Somewhere in the hold, he hears a poor shade get seasick. He hears others around that soul commit violence against him. Doing his best to hold his own, his thoughts turn. He thinks about the words on the sign over the entrance to hell. *I refuse to give up hope; to give into despair. Since the Messias has not yet come, I will continue to hope he can save me from an eternity in the underworld.* He turns his restricted view upward, and then, seeing nothing but dirty, aged wood through the gap in his hood, leans his head back against the bulkhead. The boat pitches and rocks in the river currents.

May Elohim remember me here and be gracious to me on that day. He thinks, desperately clinging to his little flame of hope. Unexpectedly, his thoughts turn to his friend Cælius. *I should have said more on the shore in Cæsarea. I should have spoken more boldly of*

God so I might spare him from a fate such as mine. Ioannes lowers his head back down and in the darkness, he whispers, "I hope God finds you, my friend, before you suffer as I do."

Chapter 4: From Soldier to Sailor

A meeting is taking place in a private room in the Antonia Fortress. Cælius pleads his case with his Centurion, who is a weathered, but fit man in his mid-30s. Because this is an informal meeting set in the garrison, the Centurion, proud but not arrogant, is not in full uniform, yet he carries himself upright as he walks back and forth. The Centurion's hands clasp a scroll behind his back and his gaze is straight ahead as he paces. He thoughtfully listens to what Cælius has to say, though he seems annoyed by the request.

Cælius stands still, at the position of attention as he makes his request. He has thought deeply about Ioannes' words in Cæsarea and they spur him on in his request to leave the legion and become a Marinus. "I cannot help it, sir, this longing to return to the sea. The call to make this change is great, which is why I request reassignment to the Praetorian Fleet."

"Yes, yes, I know, you love the sea; you've only said so 20 times. Cælius, you have pestered me with this request too many times, almost daily since we arrived in Hierosolyma." He exhales, and then continues, "You're right. I cannot understand why you would make such a request. What you're asking for, discharge from the Legion to serve in the navy, it's…" He pauses, "it's a demotion!"

"Yes sir, I know it is perceived as much, but I will still be serving Rome, just as a Marinus instead."

The Centurion stops in front of Cælius and turns to face him directly. He presents the scroll he has been carrying behind him, finally acquiescing, "Well, it would appear fortune smiles upon you Cælius. I received word there is a marinus on a ship in Cæsarea seeking the glory of a legionnaire. An exchange then; him for you." The Centurion hands him the scroll.

Cælius, restraining his excitement, accepts it with courtesy. The Centurion places his right hand on Cælius' left shoulder. "He is already on his way. Gather your things, you leave immediately. You are to report to the Centurion on the Navis Prætoria Pax in Cæsarea in two days."

"Yes sir! Thank you!"

"You're a good soldier Cælius. Your actions in the ambush were noble. We will miss you." The Centurion releases his shoulder and then turns to walk away. However, he turns back abruptly. Offering a brotherly, and somewhat mischievous, smile he says, "Oh, and one piece of advice... don't drown." He offers his hand: Cælius clasps his forearm firmly, and the Centurion his, and they shake. Upon release, Cælius strikes his chest in salute.

"May Neptunus protect you." The Centurion offers. "Now get out!" He adds with humor, shaking his head. Cælius rushes out of his office and goes to gather his things.

* * * * *

It's been two days and Cælius is happily returning to Cæsarea by way of the Via Maris. He carries his shield and spear in his left hand. Slung over his right shoulder is a small bag containing a few personal items. He strides with purpose, and anticipation, as he nears the city.

It has been a great journey thus far. He thinks. *I cannot wait to reach the sea!* He has dwelt upon his friend Ioannes, and his living God for much of the way. *How little I knew of them both. Yet, here I am, changing my entire life with the idea of honoring my friend and seeking out the one true God.*

So many emotions, and conflicts, tumble through his heart and mind. He wonders, *Have I made the right decision? Can I make the transition to life in the fleet after my service as a soldier?* Despite the uncertainty, Cælius has learned to trust his instincts, his intuition. Of course, he feels some trepidation; however, he is also confident he has made the right choice; the choice to follow his conscience and discover the God Ioannes knew.

Cælius stops for a moment with the city in full view. Its sandstone buildings set against the blue sea are a welcoming sight. He lifts his head skyward, breathing deeply of the salty sea air carried by an ocean breeze. In the distance, he hears the dull roar of ocean tide crashing gently on rock and sand. Seagulls gliding in the sky above him lift his spirits. A youthful exuberance swells within him. He resumes his pace and enters the fledgling city with great anticipation.

Walking confidently through the bustling city streets, he finds food and drink at a crowded market. He then finds a place to rest for a short time to enjoy his small meal before heading to the harbor and his new ship.

Cælius walks along the deep-water harbor noting minor work that still needs to be done before the port's official dedication. There are quite a few ships moored in the new harbor. Cælius stops to ask a man for directions. The man points toward a trireme ship moored nearby. Cælius approaches the sentries at the gangplank. He produces the scroll given to him by his former Centurion and is permitted to board the ship.

She is a beautiful two-tone, brown-colored ship. Her upper hull and superstructure are dark brown, while her lower hull is light brown wood. The two tones are separated by a white stripe, which is adorned with ruby-red, round Parma shields. Adorned with golden wings and arrows, and spaced perfectly down her side, the shields glint in the sun. A cheerful eye adorns her prow just below the stripe, while the ornate prow itself curls up and to the stern. Her white sails are furled, and a polished bronze ram glints just below the water on her bow. From a distance she appears to be a majestic queen, wearing a ruby and pearl-laden crown, peering above the surface of the sea to greet humanity. On her stern is an arched, red and white striped ceremonial tent, which has been set up for dignitaries and official business. Cælius makes his way there and then stands at attention before a table placed in the shade beneath it. He holds his scutum shield in his left hand on the deck and his spear in his right, also resting on the deck, but with the spear tip pointing out to his right, away from the naval Centurion, who is seated behind the table.

The Centurion is similar in age to his previous one. He is clean-shaven, has a fresh haircut, and, except for his helmet, which sits upon the table, is wearing the full regalia of his post. He quietly reads the orders on the scroll produced by Cælius, occasionally looking up at him. The ship's Optio stands just behind and to the left of Centurion. He inspects Cælius more closely.

The Centurion rolls up the scroll, lightly drops it on his desk, and stands. "Well then Cælius," he begins, "I was a bit surprised to learn a legionnaire such as you would want to become a marinus. This is often considered a step down from your lofty position as a soldier of Rome."

He states with some sarcasm. "Why have you made such a request?"

"I wish to be back on the sea sir. I... missed it. If I may be so bold, my humble wish is to serve Rome in a way in which I too can be fulfilled."

The Centurion tilts his head slightly and raises his right eyebrow. He glances at the Optio, who gives him an expressionless look before moving around the right side of the table and to Cælius' left. He surprises the former soldier with a hearty laugh and a slap on the back. A little stunned by this move Cælius turns his head to look at the Centurion. The Optio moves toward the desk takes the scroll and begins to tidy up.

"Ha, ha, ha! Good answer. Welcome aboard Cælius! Truly, I am happy to have a battle-tested legionnaire such as yourself onboard. I have no doubt you will make a great marinus."

"Thank you," Cælius says cautiously. "I am not accustomed to such greetings. You are much too gracious."

"Ah, well, that's because you're used to legionnaires."

"If I may sir, as you say, I have been on land for a long time, it may take me a while to get used to the movement of the sea under my feet again."

The Centurion pats him on the back again and laughs. This time though he also steers him out of the tent into the open air. He teaches Cælius about the ship as they walk. "Come, let me tell you about our lady, Pax, explain your duties, and introduce you to some of your shipmates."

Walking at a slow pace in the sun, the ship's captain continues, "She is both a diplomatic vessel and a cargo ship. Our squadron, Classis Alexandrina, makes its home berth in Egypt. We were sent here to Cæsarea Maritima for the dedication of the deep-water port, which was built by the Iudæus King Herod; his tribute to Augustus Caesar." His gregarious nature revealed, he winks at Cælius denoting his pride in receiving the tribute on behalf of Caesar. He then continues his instruction, "Once all the pomp and circumstance of the dedication is over, we will embark upon our mission of escorting spice and grain shipments from here, and from Alexandria, back to Peninsula Italia. There we sometimes pick up Legionnaires and transport them back here."

"Now, as you probably already know, most piracy has been quelled on the Mare Internum; they know better than to provoke the wrath of our fleet." Again, he pats Cælius on the back and gives him a nod of confidence. "However, you are here in case we do find them, or any other threat."

"Now, as for your duties." He says more seriously. "There are no roads or fortifications to build, instead you will help maintain our vessel. She's a fine ship, worthy to ply the waters of Neptunus! I expect you to defend her with your life and to help keep her seaworthy. As a matter of fact, you will be standing guard this very night. It will be an opportunity for you to get to know her."

They approach another Marinus standing near the seaward side of the ship with shield and spear in hand. He is roughly the same age as Cælius and is dressed in full armor. "Ah, Marcus! This is Cælius, our newest marinus. He is our legionnaire transfer, so it should be easy for you to train him. You're both standing the watch tonight. Marcus, I expect you will familiarize him with the ship."

"Aye, sir. Come Cælius, we'll start our rounds at the bow."

"Good man. Good man." Says the Centurion as he turns to take his leave.

The two marinus turn and walk toward the bow talking. Marcus asks, "So, why the request for reassignment? There is already much speculation among the crew."

Cælius thinks it wise not to mention the answers he seeks about the Iudæus God, instead, he provides the same reasons he gave his former, and new, Centurion. These explanations satisfy Marcus too, as they begin the tour of the ship.

* * * * *

Later that evening, Marcus and Cælius are standing near the stern on the seaward side of the ship. It's sunset and there is a slight ocean breeze. Marcus asks, "I'm going below to make a round. You will be okay up here, yes?"

"Yes. I'll meet you at the bow ladder."

Marcus turns and walks toward the stern ladder leading below. Cælius lingers near the railing, staring out at the ocean. Glistening, blue waters gently rise and fall. White and gray gulls glide on salty ocean breezes in twilight skies. The once-white clouds have begun to turn different shades of vermillion, purple, and orange. After enjoying this simple beauty for a moment, he turns, crosses over to the port side of the ship, and then continues his patrol.

On the port side, a torchlit Cæsarea; flames twisting, flickering, and casting shadows against the white stone buildings. Like the last time he was here, there is revelry in the streets. He pauses near the gangway for a moment and nods at the sentries standing below on the dock. Gazing out at the city, he mutters to himself, "Last time I was the one celebrating. A part of me still wants to roam the streets for wine, women, and food too. Hmmm...those habits will be hard to break, I think... It may be a long night. God, if you are indeed present, I ask you to guide me and to quell the lust in my heart."

Marcus climbs the ladder and steps out on the main deck. "What? Did you say something?"

Cælius is a little caught off guard. "No, nothing. Just commenting on my new perspective of the city."

"Ah, yes." Marcus agrees. "I too would like to join in the revelry. Not tonight I'm afraid. Not tonight." His voice trails off. The two continue to stand their watch. They swap stories of adventures and battles, talking about different towns and ports, faring sea storms and dust storms, and of life at sea and in the legion.

Chapter 5: Skewed Judgement

Charon's ferry runs aground hard and fast on the other side of the River Styx. It jolts as the keel slides up a gravel bank and meets with solid rock causing some crewmen and demonic escorts to heave forward at the sudden stop. Charon gives a hearty laugh as some of his 'passengers' fall before instantly changing to a foul mood. He curses, "Bloody rowers!" And shouts at everyone within earshot, "Get the damned off my ship!"

Dæmons rush the cargo hold, fling open the hatch, and begin gleefully plucking souls from below. Some are pushed indiscriminately down the gangplank while some are led in a semi-orderly fashion. Others are brutally cast overboard. Ioannes is one of those cast over the side.

Still hooded, he is drug out of the hold by the chains on his wrists, led to the railing, and then shoved over the side. He lands on the shore with his bare back on land and his feet in the water. He writhes in pain on the forsaken shore. The unnamed soul is also cast over, making a large splash next to Ioannes.

Goblin dæmons fly over the rails. Flapping their leathery wings, they slowly descend and land around the two shades. Dæmon Captain strolls nonchalantly down the gangway to collect his quarry. The goblin dæmons stand them up, chain them together, and prepare them to be escorted down a rougher road into hell.

Dæmon Captain wrests the lead chain from one of the lesser dæmons and gives a yank, prompting Ioannes and his compatriot to follow. They limp out of the water and up the rocky beach, moving on to the next road.

Inland, the terrain changes. Gone is any feeling of moisture from the river. This new road is like a dry, desert mountain region. Rocks cast shadows from an eerie, gray light in the background. The group follows the winding road, their pace slowing as a line forms.

Ioannes cannot see the malevolent outcropping of rock ahead, which in itself is a small blessing. It's a kind of stone amphitheater. A makeshift platform has been carved from the dark brown stone in the center, with an archway leading downward into the further depths of hell on the left. A single demon reclines on a large curule chair in the middle of the platform. Perched in various places above him are gray-winged dæmons glaring at the souls passing through the judgment seat of hell. They glare at passing shades like gargoyles, waiting to devour any one of them who dares an escape.

Dæmon Captain is reluctantly patient as he herds his souls forward, grumbling and passively cursing until he reaches the front of the line. There he stops his procession and waits to be called forward by the dæmon 'judge'.

Although his clothes are stained and soiled with ash and burn marks, the vainglorious judge is dressed in what were once the finest Roman robes. A civic crown made with small fig leaves encircles two, smaller horns upon his head. He reclines lazily on an ornate curule chair carved from opaque bone.

A massive arm rough carved out of the stone above reaches out over him. Its hand grips a jagged, and rusty, iron scale. Both bowls, filled with flame, hang from soot-covered chains. The left bowl dips lower than the right one denoting skewed justice and favoring the archway leading downward.

It is easy to see this judge fashions himself as a haughty Roman governor or a pompous senator. With an uninterested sigh, he lazily motions for the next sinner to come forward, sighing, "Bring forward the next offender." Dæmon Captain grins, unchains Ioannes, and half drags him to the platform. There he quickly drives Ioannes to his knees. The wicked justice asks, "Are you not going to remove his hood?"

"He is not worthy to look upon this fine court."

The judge sighs again. "Very well. Proceed with your accusations dæmon."

The Dæmon Captain begins, "This man is not only a terrible soldier; he refused to fight or take the life of his enemy. He did nothing in service to his 'empire' but carry a banner and cook meals. He is a coward!" He laughs heartily. "He was not a good son either; often disobeying his family's wishes, rejecting our *beloved* Roman gods, associating with Iudæus slaves, and seeking out our enemy, the one, true God. He is a traitor to his family and is an unprofitable servant to the same, living God he claims to follow. Ha! This wretch could not even openly commit to serving El Yisrael."

There is a slight pause, and then Ioannes drops his head down toward his knees, a sudden sense of guilt and shame overcomes him. He knows more of his sins, his iniquities, even the hidden ones, are about to be laid bare. Dæmon Captain grins widely before continuing, "Oh, the things he did in his youth before attempting to serve his God. Unable to control his hunger, he stole food from a market. Unable to control his lust, he snuck out of his home to visit a lupanar, wantonly laying with prostitutes. Desiring to keep these and other sins hidden, he has lied. By his actions, he either allowed or brought, evil into the world. Now he thinks God will spare him; rescue him. No!" He spits toward Ioannes. "He deserves punishment."

An uneasy silence fills the air. Dæmon Captain looks expectantly at the judge as he deliberates. Ioannes thinks to himself, *I am a liar, a thief, and a fornicator; indeed, the things I have done in my youth justify my sentence. Still, I hope; beyond all hope, that I have done more virtuous things in my adult life out of love for Elohim, and that the Messias, the true judge of the world, might yet find me... even here.*

The arrogant judge again waives his hand dismissively and moans, "I agree. Take him to Limbo for now. There you can bind and abandon him until we decide which circle of hell best suits him. The lower-level scum will retrieve him at the appropriate time."

Dæmon Captain nods, and then drags the hooded Ioannes back to be chained once more. His unwilling companion, the unnamed soul, resists being unchained at first. He has heard Ioannes' judgment and knows what is to come. However, he too is forcefully drug to the platform and driven to his knees. The false judge yawns with boredom, "And this one?"

The unnamed soul does not think he should be judged. Cursing loudly through clenched teeth, he insults, "Worms and maggots consume you!" Though hooded as well, he then lunges in the direction of the judge's voice. Startled, the judge gasps as he jumps to his feet. The gargoyle dæmons rattle their wings and scrape claws on the stone above the platform eager to descend upon the offender. Dæmon Captain instantly grabs the unnamed soul, throws him to the ground, and begins beating him.

The judge collects himself, raises his hand to stay the gargoyle dæmons, and then haughtily steps down from the platform. He moves close to the Unnamed Soul, "You dare?!" exclaims the enraged judge through gnashed teeth. "Take him to Limbo as well... for now." Dæmon Captain restrains him, holding him down on his knees. The evil magistrate leans down next to Unnamed Soul's ear and, in a vicious tone, hisses through the burlap hood. "I know which circle is suitable for you. I will contact your torturer personally, you disease-ridden criminal. I want to be there when he drags you, kicking and screaming, deeper into hell. You will wait in Limbo in anticipation of our arrival."

The judge gathers his dirty robes and strolls arrogantly back to his comfortable chair proclaiming, "Now get him out of my sight and bring the next one before me!"

Satisfied with the outcome, Dæmon Captain drags Unnamed Soul back and chains him to Ioannes. Taking the lead chain, he gives a yank to let them know to move forward. They are then led through the archway like bulls to slaughter. The gargoyles scratch at the rock and hiss as they watch the condemned pass through the arch where everything becomes dark.

It isn't long before the pageantry of the Cæsarea Maritima port dedication is over, and the crew of the Pax is finally underway to Alexandria. Cælius stands near the bow as they head out to sea. He relishes the simple pleasures presented to his senses. The wind and ocean spray on his face. The sound of creaking oars as they splash into the water and take strain. The white sail unfurled and filled with the wind. The awareness of a rolling sea underfoot. It all brings back fond, childhood memories of fishing near the coast with his father. This day, the day he returned to the sea, is the happiest he has been in quite some time.

Days at sea come and go. Yes, there is always work to be done, scrubbing the main deck, coiling lines, and watches to be stood, but life at sea is good; and oh, the sights. The Pharos Lighthouse; its great beacon calling out from miles away. Rowing into Mandrákion Harbor where the Colossus of Rhodes once stood. Though he marvels at these wonders of man, his thoughts often turn to Adonai. *If man can create such wonderous things as these, what majestic things might the one true God be capable of?* He thinks. The growing thirst for knowledge of God completely changes his port calls over the next two years.

As his faith grows, his habits began to change as well. Instead of seeking out the usual vice with shipmates, Cælius spends many port calls, especially in the Iudæa province, quietly seeking out teachers willing to instruct him in Elohim's ways. He learns different lessons each time, and the frequent escorts between Cæsarea, Alexandria, and Peninsula Italia afford him much time to contemplate this new knowledge.

It isn't always easy to find a rabbi willing to teach him, but he manages to connect with a handful who were happy to teach God's commandments, how to pray, what the prophets of old accomplished, as well as the coming of the Messias. He even discovers a couple of Ioannes' former teachers.

While on another voyage back to Cæsarea, Cælius patrols the ship. He stops at the bow to feel the fresh sea spray on his face; to him it never gets old. There he reflects on the reason he became a soldier. *For discipline and glory.* He thinks. *Now Elohim has led me back to the sea, to my new life on this ship. I must discern what he has in store for my future.*

The change in his behavior is not lost on his shipmates either. He becomes aware of a slight mistrust forming among the other marinus. As Cælius turns and walks astern, he moves past Marcus and two other marinus standing next to the mast. They watch him go by silently and then begin speaking again after he passes. Cælius cannot hear what they say, he is still too deep in his thoughts.

He ponders a predicament, *Legionnaires and Marinus are supposed to be loyal to the emperor and no other. That loyalty is usually demonstrated by offering a sacrifice to him if promoted to the rank of centurion. This violates Adonai's first commandment and puts me in a dangerous position. The more I learn and the closer I come to God, the greater the danger becomes of being found out. I could be thrown into the ocean and left to drown if my centurion, optio, or other marinus knew of my ongoing conversion in faith.* Cælius looks over his shoulder toward the sea as he walks.

His secret port call activities and cloistered life onboard the ship are mostly tolerated as eccentric though, and life at sea goes on a bit longer without issue... for the time being.

* * * * *

On this day, the ship is moored in the port of Andriake in Anatolia. Most of the crew is making their way ashore and walking up the road into the city of Myra. Marcus, Cælius, and a couple of newer marinus are standing on the main deck, discussing their plans for the evening. The two new marinus are younger than Marcus and Cælius. Cassius is 20, and Felix is only 19 years old.

Marcus states, "We will be sailing for Seleucia Pieria tomorrow, and then on to Cæsarea. Since we don't have watch tonight, I say we all head into town to indulge in the pleasures of wine, women, and feasting. What say you?" He asks as he gestures to the group.

Cælius responds first, "Thank you, Marcus, for the invitation but I think I'll pass." Cassius and Felix look curiously at him.

"You haven't been out with us in a very long time Cælius, surely you miss the revelry?" Inquires Cassius

"Why do you hold yourself apart from us?" Asks Marcus. "You think yourself superior because you were once a Legionnaire?"

"No, not at all. I only prefer a smaller meal close to the ship and a respite. Truly, I appreciate your invitation, but I wish to enjoy a quieter evening before we sail tomorrow."

Marcus, snubbed by perceived rejection, shrugs his shoulders and turns to the other two marinus, "Come on then, who else is going?"

Cassius, "I'm in. Let's get into town before the rowers do."

Felix, "I need to stow my gear. Head on in, I'll find you."

Marcus huffs, turns, and heads for the gangplank; Cassius walks along with him. Cælius watches them leave. Felix, still politely observing Cælius, asks abruptly, "I know I haven't been onboard as long as you and Marcus, but I can see there is something different in the way you carry yourself, compared to the rest of the crew, Cælius. You certainly have a pride in you but are much too humble and kind for a former Legionnaire. We're all just trying to figure out what has brought this about in you."

Cælius turns to look at the young sailor. He offers a smile of gratitude with a pat on his shoulder, "Maybe one day soon I will tell you the source of what you see in me, young man. Now, you better hurry off or your shipmates will drink the wineskins dry before you get there."

Felix nods and then goes to ready himself for a night ashore.

Dusk has overtaken the Andriakian Harbor. Cælius cloaks himself in a plain, cream-colored toga, covering his uniform. He acknowledges the sentries as he steps off the gangplank onto shore, and then pulls a length of his toga up over his head. He looks around and then begins to walk toward a small housing area toward the back of the port, which is downhill from the city of Myra. As he walks through a tiny market, two Roman soldiers, with red togas concealing their identities begin to follow him.

Cælius stops at a house and knocks. An older, bearded man, dressed in a simple tunic, opens the door. The old rabbi smiles at him, and then motions for him to come in. Cælius again takes a brief look around; he does not see the two soldiers standing down the alley.

He enters and then closes the door behind him. The two soldiers watching him from a distance remove the togas from their heads and are revealed to be Marcus and Cassius. Marcus puts his hand to his chin and strokes it, "Hmmm? I wonder whom Cælius meets with?"

Cassius is agitated and frustrated from having to spy on a fellow marinus instead of carousing in town. "I told you, it's no one. Let's go, Marcus, I want wine and women."

Marcus snaps out of his contemplative stare and slaps his shipmate on the shoulder. "You are right young man. I have held us up far too long. Let's see what this little town has to offer us, yes?" The two turn and head toward Myra.

* * * * *

The next day the Pax, which is at full sail, plies through the waters surrounded by the other ships in the squadron. Cælius stands near the rail staring out at the deep blue waters glistening under the bright sun. He hears footprints and turns to see Marcus casually approaching him. "Quiet night then Cælius?" He asks.

Cælius turns to look back out at the sea. "Dinner with old friends. It was nice to see them again."

"You have friends in Myra? How is that possible?" Though he seems nonchalant, there is an accusatory tone in Marcus' voice.

Cælius' response is guarded but he remains honest. "They were good to a legionnaire brother of mine when we marched to Cæsarea a couple of years ago. Since we were in Andriake, I thought I would pass on good tidings. They offered dinner and I could not refuse."

Marcus steps closer to Cælius with a suspicious, and slightly irritated, look on his face as if to warn or threaten him. The exchange, however, is abruptly interrupted by shouting coming from the stern of the ship.

Having just rounded the Carpasian peninsula of Cyprus, the island can still be seen in the distance as the two men look astern. A dark, malevolent storm has come to life north of the peninsula. It is moving directly toward the squadron as if purposefully seeking them out. A massive gray and white squall line has already stretched out across the sky ahead of it.

Marcus turns back to give Cælius a hard stare. Their duties overtake their issues and then they both run toward the main mast. They lash their shields and spears to it and then help other crewmen lower the main sail. High clouds move in overhead, darkening the sky, and creating an ominous shadow over the ship as they work.

Chapter 7: Abandoned

The condemned procession emerges from a short, dark tunnel amidst a group of sulfur vents. Yellow stains cover dark, blackish-red stalagmites venting light gray smoke into a dark, almost black sky. The once smooth, wide road has become a more treacherous path. The ground is hot, jagged, and harsher. Ioannes and the Unnamed Soul are led down a twisting side trail away from other shades moving downward. Here everything is much darker than before; an eerie firelight dimly illuminates the sky.

They only walk a short distance before Dæmon Captain abruptly halts in a small open area. He quietly points to two eyelets anchored in rock on the ground about 20 feet apart. He drops the lead chain and growls, "Stooop! We are here slaves."

That is the extent of his courtesy as he immediately shoves Ioannes to the ground on his belly and steps on his back with one foot. Goblin dæmons pull the chain from his shackles and connect them to an eye anchored in the black, gritty rock. Once chained, the goblin dæmons loosen his hood and step back.

Dæmon Captain reaches down, and painfully yanks the burlap hood off his head, scraping his face as he pulls it off. He then removes his foot from Ioannes' back, who wearily rolls to his side and glances up to finally see his imprisoner. Dæmon Captain immediately strikes him in the face with the back of his hand and then spits in his face.

Ioannes keeps one eye closed so the spittle will not run into it. He looks slowly around. After all this time, his captors are revealed. The smaller, goblin-like dæmons are all roughly 5-foot-tall with average human builds. They have bat-like wings on their backs, some tucked down, and others stretched out behind them. Their skin color is a reddish/tan color, they are 'naked', but have no genitalia. The hair on their head is wild and matted, but short, with two small horns protruding from their foreheads. They carry chains, shackles, or a slender, two-pronged, skewer-like pitchfork, which is as long as they are tall.

The Dæmon Captain appears black against the dark sky, but his skin has a blue shimmer. He stands nearly seven feet tall and, except for his pudgy belly, is very muscular. Red irises blaze through otherwise black eyes. A haughty smirk spreads across his battle-scarred face. He carries a large, cruel-looking, single-blade axe in his left hand, while his right hovers over a Whip on his belt. He wears black and dark brown barbarian armor, with a black, spiked pauldron on his left shoulder. Small, ivory-colored horns protrude around his bald head as if they were a spiked crown.

Through his grotesque smile, he hisses, "You think you lived a virtuous life did you not?" A deep, guttural chortle slips past the yellowish, dagger-like teeth. "Heh, heh, heh. You are a sinner. God does not love you, worm."

With a sudden swift motion, he pulls the whip from his side and cracks it across Ioannes' side and back, splitting his skin. Ash, stirred up from the whip, immediately mingles with the blood and stings. Ioannes wails in both physical and spiritual pain. "Deus meus[11], why have you forsaken me?!"

"Shut up! God is the one who sent you here, fool." He swiftly kicks Ioannes in the head. "I told you to abandon hope." He takes pleasure in watching his victim roll to his side in pain.

---

[11] "My God" (translated from Latin)

"Go on wretch, despair, for you are a great sinner who does not deserve to be in the presence of God. There is no rest, no peace for you here."

Dæmon Captain then grinds his hot, sandaled foot into the open wound on Ioannes' side making it open further and burn more fiercely. He laughs with hearty satisfaction. All the other, goblin dæmons skulking about in the shadows join in with their incessant cackling. Ioannes curls up on his side on the bare, black stone; the shackles cutting into his wrists. Dæmon Captain waives a dismissive hand at him. "Bah! Leave the whelp to his despair."

He then turns his sights on the Unnamed Soul. A malevolent grin again spreads across his face as he stares down at his prey. He motions for the goblin dæmons to bind him to the ground and remove his hood.

Dæmon Captain places his axe on the ground and secures his whip to his side while they carry out his orders. Once he can see, the still angry Unnamed Soul kicks at one of the smaller dæmons. Without a word the Dæmon Captain pounces on him, unleashing his fury, and beating him severely.

Afterward, he stands upright and takes a step back, breathing heavily from his assault. The Unnamed Soul is barely conscious, laying limp on the ground. "Truly... [pant] I... [pant] enjoyed that." He reaches for his axe, and then motions to his squad of dæmons to go. He secures his axe to the armor on his back, kick's ash at Unnamed Soul, and then turns to leave. "Let's go find more! HA, HA, HA!"

The demonic band walks away. Ioannes stirs. He wipes the blood, spittle, and ash from his swollen eye using his forearm, and then painfully rises to his knees to survey his surroundings. The hellscape is brought into full view.

There is no sky, just black, stale air. Billowing, gray clouds, moving fluidly like a shadowy, turbulent thunderstorm, fill the space overhead. The rock too is a black and burgundy color. The only light comes from a red-orange glow of what looks like several lava flows emanating from a lake of fire or cauldron of lava near a vast chasm. Glowing embers and big flakes of gray ash fall sporadically from the ebony tempest. The landscape resembles a slowly erupting volcano seen just after dusk.

Ioannes glances at his counterpart chained nearby but can only see his back in the firelight. Unnamed Soul suddenly twists and turns with rage as a large, burning ember land on him. He curses through gnashed teeth as it burns his skin. Ioannes whispers to himself, "Oh, Adonai, how long must I remain here? Will you come for me? Or will you allow me to be dragged deeper into the pit? Deus meus, salva mea[12]."

---

[12] "My God, save me." (translated from Latin)

Chapter 8: Drowning in Sin

The wicked tempest churns and boils, moving swiftly toward the squadron of ships. Ahead of the squall line, the sea turns violent. Waves rise and fall, breaking across the bow, and tossing the Pax about like a piece of driftwood. Shouts of fear erupt when gale force broadside the ship with such power as to push it into the crashing waves. Rowers have manned their oars and worked desperately to not only keep the ship stable but also plying forward through the angry sea.

The ominous white squall line, highlighted by the ark green and gray sky behind it, blows over the ship, blotting out the sun entirely. An eerie feeling fills the hearts of Cælius and other crewmen, who keep glancing out past the bow watching the blue sky disappear behind the shadowy, turbulent edge of the storm. Lightning flashes furiously overhead, crackling and sizzling. A massive boom of thunder sounds. It shakes the planks of the ship before rumbling across the dark, rain-laden sky. The thunderclap bursts the clouds, releasing a torrent upon them.

Having secured all the equipment he can, Cælius rushes forward to the port side of the bow edge to brace himself. Marcus is already there, clutching the starboard rail and shouting a fearful prayer, "Oh Neptunus, we beg you, calm the waters! Save us from this tempest."

Cassius and Felix join them as the boat pitches and rolls in the swelling sea. The Pax crests a massive wave and dives, bow first, into raging waters. Ocean spray crashes over the bow and soaks everyone gathered there. Cælius, calmer than the others, instinctively calls out but not to the Roman god Neptunus... "Adonai, I fear your wrath. Please, Father of us all, spare this crew from your anger; save us from this tempest."

Suddenly the same trepidation the young Ioannes had in Cæsarea overcomes him. He knows he just prayed out loud. Cælius looks up toward Marcus and the others. Water pours from their faces as their stares meet. Lightning flashes and thunder rumbles. Still clutching the rail, Marcus shouts, "You! This tempest is your fault! You have forsaken the gods and brought the fury of Neptunus upon us!" He turns to the other two marinus and orders, "Throw him over the side! His death will please Neptunus and he will calm the sea."

Cælius turns and slides his right foot, opening his stance and bracing his back against the rail. Marcus, Cassius, and a hesitant Felix cautiously move toward their shipmate. Gripping the railing with his left hand, Cælius instinctively reaches across his body and places his right hand on the handle of his gladius. He does not wish to fight his fellow countrymen but knows he must defend himself if necessary.

There is no time for a confrontation though. The bow begins to rise as the ship moves at an angle up a large wave. Cælius notices the faces of the marinus approaching him grow pale. Cassius points at something behind him shouts something inaudible, and then he and Felix rush back to their side of the railing. Marcus, with gladius in hand and standing just in front of Cælius, freezes in terror.

Cælius looks over his shoulder and sees the unthinkable. The Victoria, one of her sister ships in the squadron, had been turned by a rogue wave and is bearing straight for the Pax. There is no doubt they will be sunk by her ram.

Cælius grabs the railing with both arms and braces for the impact.

The Victoria slams into the side of the Pax, breaking her main mast. Its ram pierces the hull just behind the corvus[13]. The impact thrusts the Pax sideways into another wave. Cælius nearly loses his grip from the shock of the collision. The hull splinters and brakes; rowers below deck scream in horror. The massive wave they once plied crashes down upon the damaged deck, completely shattering the ship in two. Water floods inward; the ship begins to quickly break apart and sink into the stormy deep. Utter chaos ensues as crewmen fall or jump into the raging sea.

The bow of the ship, which Cælius held firm to, turns downward due to the heavy ram on its prow. He looks around and notices Marcus is gone, swept into the sea. The two younger Marinus are jumping blindly into the water. The bow of the ship raises in the air which gives Cælius just enough visibility of the wreckage around him. He spots a large chuck of hull nearby and leaps toward it, plunging into the briny waters. He quickly surfaces, swims

---

[13] Naval boarding weapon near the bow.

through debris to the chunk of wood, and pulls himself up on the makeshift raft.

Catching his breath and looking around, Cælius sees the Victoria capsize under the weight of the wave that broke the Pax in two. He also notices several crewmen bobbing up and down in the stormy waters desperately trying to keep their heads above water. Some of the rowers cling to bits of their paddles, while others frantically search for something to cling to. He knows he must save them.

Searching for something to help, he spies a length of rope trailing from the piece of hull he lay upon. He grasps it, pulling all of it up to his raft. He ties off the tethered end, making sure it is secure. Discarding his belt and gladius into the ocean, he then ties the loose end around his waist.

He is about to jump in when an unexpected thought enters his mind. He remembers his friend, the Andriakian rabbi, and the lesson of the previous evening. Cælius learned about God's willingness to cleanse the Assyrian commander Naaman of his leprosy in the Jordan River. Deep down, he was envious of Naaman. He too had hoped to make a pilgrimage to the same river one day to be cleansed of his iniquities in its waters. He wonders if the Mare Internum will do now instead.

Momentarily dwelling on this thought, a sense of calm overcomes him. He turns his eyes skyward. The rain falls upon his face. "God in heaven, is this to be my baptism? Might I be purified in these waters? If so, Adonai, grant me the strength to save as many of my shipmates as you will. In this, I trust in you."

He returns his focus to the turbulent sea and searches for the closest man. Taking a deep breath, he dives in. He swims stridently to the first man. Bobbing and sputtering, he shouts, "Grab onto me! I will pull you to safety!"

Without a word, the rower quickly obeys and grasps the collar of his armor. Cælius uses the line to pull them both back to the raft. Once the rower is safe, he swims back out for another, and then another. In all, he pulls four of his shipmates to safety.

Fatigue, however, is setting in. When he goes out for a fifth, exhaustion overtakes him. The weight of his waterlogged clothes and breastplate pulls him downward. Not only is he unable to reach the fifth sailor, but he also now struggles to keep his head above water.

Fear of dying causes panic. Choking and gasping for air, he flails about in the choppy water before finally sinking beneath the waves, unseen by the ones he saved. He tries desperately to hold his breath but cannot. The saltwater fills his nostrils causing him to gag and breath in more. His arms and legs fail; he has no strength left.

Still tethered to the debris, but sinking deeper, he looks toward the surface. He hears the muffled sounds of screaming, timber bursting, and thunder rumbling across the sky. Those he saved are too weary to notice him. Fleeting thoughts pass through his mind. *Is this... Is this what sinners drowning in the great flood experienced? Was this... their final view... of Noah's ark?*

His vision blurs. He barely recognizes the bolt of lightning flashing across an unreachable sky. It sheds just enough light to silhouette several feet and legs surrounding the makeshift raft he is tethered to. Then, there is nothing more, no sound, no sight, no thought, only the silence of the darkest deep. The once-blue waters of the Mare Internum have swallowed him whole.

Chapter 9: Cursed Waters

The hellscape once again comes into focus. Blue lightning streaks through the distant volcanic maelstrom above the lake of fire. Ioannes rests on his legs in a kneeling position with his head down. The cut on his left side, from the dæmon's whip, has cauterized but is still raw. Dark purple bruises cover his body, and blisters from falling embers have risen in various places. He has only enough chains to either sit or rise to his knees; he cannot stand.

He raises his eyes to the distant, churning fires; great wailing noises echo across the barren landscape. They are drowned out only by his thoughts, *how long have I been chained here? How long have I listened to sounds of violence, of wailing and weeping?* The once-youthful features of his face have sunken. His lips have split and cracked; he licks at them to no avail. His throat is parched; not even his saliva can ease the dryness when he swallows.

He begins to look around slowly and aimlessly, thinking, *this abandonment, this torment, and pain, it is maddening. The temptation to despair, to give in to the darkness, weighs heavy on me. Thoughts of hopelessness, that there is no way out of this place, constantly plague me.* He feels disorientation setting in. *How long have I been here? Days, months, years?* He sighs out loud. *There is no knowing in the scope of eternity.*

Ioannes continues to search his surroundings when he realizes Unnamed Soul is sitting on his buttocks with crossed legs and looking in his general direction. He seems to be peering through Ioannes to some far-off place. His face and body appear far worse than Ioannes'. Scars long before coming here cover his face and torso. His appearance is quickly overlooked as Ioannes perks up at the prospect of having a conversation. "How long do you think we've been here friend?"

Unnamed Soul's head turns ever so slightly, and his intense focus lands on Ioannes. He shouts through clenched teeth. "Friend?! I am NOT your friend! Were you not listening? We've been sent here for eternity. Time no longer matters. Stultus[14]!" His irritation, hatred, and contempt are palpable; they're reflected in his body language and his words.

---

[14] Stupid or fool (translated from Latin)

Ioannes is taken aback by it but keeps his calm demeanor. Desperately trying to keep his sanity in the tumultuous surroundings, he continues the conversation, "I know you think me a fool. Though I cannot explain why I still have hope Elohim or his Messias, might still save me, us, before we descended any further."

Unnamed Soul snorts in derision, "You have hope!? You're even dumber than I thought. I would kick you myself if I could reach you! Shut up. Leave me alone."

The Unnamed Soul uncomfortably turns his body and fixes his gaze on the black pit in the distance. Defeated and dejected, Ioannes drops his head in sadness. The distant wailing and churning fires once again fill his ears.

* * * * *

Somewhere close by, a large greenish-brown river flows uninterrupted. Its black sand banks bear no vegetation, only boulders of volcanic pumice and the intermittent spire of jagged obsidian. Small, blood-colored whirlpools swirl here and there streaming out burgundy eddies into the putrid waters. Unseen fires give a dim glow to the sky overhead.

Several bodies are floating in the river, and Cælius is among them. He floats on his back with arms outstretched. Only his torso and head ride above the surface; everything from his lower stomach down is underwater. He opens his eyes to the dark sky. He immediately realizes he is drifting, completely nude as it were, in the foulest of warm, muddy waters. Thinking he is still drowning; he flails about in the water before trying to swim without direction.

Coming to his senses, he stops to tread water and spits the foul-tasting liquid from his mouth. *Wait, where am I swimming to?* He thinks. Mourning and crying from all directions reach his ears. He scans the water for others, finding many. Some are treading water like him, some are trying to swim, while others just float belly up. He murmurs to himself, "What is this place?"

Then, floating by him, groaning, is the fifth rower he tried to save from his ship; the one whom he had drowned while trying to save. An awful feeling quickly fills the pit of his stomach, and his mind races. *Is this? Am I in the underworld? God did not grant me purification in the stormy waters of the Mare Internum? Why I am in this river? If I am bound for Hell, this cannot be the way. There is a road into the underworld; one must pay the boatman to cross the River Styx into the afterlife.* He pauses as he realizes the truth. *Wait! Is this the River Styx? Is this how those who die at sea enter the afterlife?*

Fear grips him. Cælius searches anxiously for a haven, again mumbling to himself, "I must get out of this horrible water." He spots a place just downriver where he can get out and try to gain his bearings. He uses the current in his favor as he swims toward it, doing his best not to get any of the filth in his mouth or nose. Small eddies push and pull his body, driving a deep sense of urgency to reach the bank.

Just as he nears the shore, a frenzy breaks out downstream. There is frantic splashing and screaming; it spreads upriver like a tidal wave of sound. Cælius does not turn to see what causes it. He closes in on the small pocket of black obsidian. The water shallows and underneath him is thick, gritty mud. It oozes under his feet and hands. Rather than trying to stand and walk through it, he stays low, pulling his naked body through the squelchy, water-lapped mire toward the bank.

There, he quickly and quietly pulls himself up on the flat stone. Sharp spires of volcanic glass form giant claws; he feels like he is sitting in the palm of some monstrous stone beast. However, the spires provide some protection from which he can catch his breath, as well as see what is causing the madness in the water. Breathing heavily, Cælius cautiously peers around one of the spires.

Three trireme ships are working their way up the river ahead of a massive, gray fog bank. The fog bank rolls like the squall of the ill-fated storm that brought him here. However, it appears to be slowly following the ships and not overtaking them. It also blankets the river and banks so he cannot see beyond it. Some of the lighter, more wispy fog dances around the glistening black hulls at the ship's water line. Separated by a green, scaled stripe, like that of a giant serpent, the upper part of their hulls is blood red in color, not black. Ragged, ebony oars reach out into the water like the legs of a centipede. Great black sails with scarlet stripes billow in an unfelt wind, likely spurred on by the malevolent fog itself.

On the prow of each ship is a great angry eye peering out into the desolate riverscape as though it is looking for fresh souls. Just above their massive, rust-colored rams but below their evil eyes, is a great open maw lined with massive spear tips for teeth. Though it does not burn the ships, an ominous fire churns within those mouths. Orange and yellow tongues of flame lick the sides of the ships as they move upriver, their salivating trail of black smoke mingling with the billowing fog to their sterns. Their prows curl upward into the shape of great, brown horns with rusty chains as rigging running from the foremast to the main mast, all the way back to the stern.

The ships stop and pull in their oars. A variety of grotesque, barnacle, and seaweed-covered dæmons carrying large boathooks, tridents, and nets man the rails. They rhythmically beat their tools on the main deck and railing, chanting and cheering in unholy synchronicity with the drumbeats echoing from below decks. Their sound reverberates through the water.

An unseen, deep, and raspy voice booms upriver, echoing along the cursed banks, "Call forth this new beast...this Kraken. Let it whet its appetite on these shades. Let us witness its power before we release it upon the world of the living."

At his command, a large demon steps forward on the lead ship. He carries a great horn, curved like that of a mouflon, except much larger. He steps to the bow and sounds the horn; its deep guttural bawl sends ripples across the surface of the river of the damned. Then the crews fall silent in anticipation of what is to come.

Though it continues to flow, the water begins to churn and bubble, like water in a hot cauldron. Random souls here and there suddenly plunge beneath the roiling waters. The source of their disappearance is quickly made known. Large tentacled arms clutching their prey burst through the river's surface. The men and women in their grasp wail, curse, and flail about as they are painfully whipped through the air and slammed down on the decks of the wicked ships. The demonic crews descend upon those souls, binding them, and thrusting them below decks.

Those that try to swim away are entangled by the unseen monsters' tentacles. Some make it to shore only to be ambushed, chained, and beaten by ghoulish hordes patrolling the banks. Others swim directly toward the ships out of fear of the creature below or the roving bands ashore. The demonic crews howl in delight as they plunge their boathooks into the water, yanking their fresh catch of shades, screaming and cursing, out of the foul waters.

Cælius sees something unexpected then. He sees a panic-stricken Marcus swimming toward him. "Help!" –He screams between gurgles– "Help me!" Before Cælius can react, Marcus plunges backward beneath the surface of the murky waters. A slimy tentacle breaks through the surface of the water only seconds later with Marcus dangling helplessly in its grip like a worm in a man's grasp.

The beast's massive brown beak rises slowly above the waterline at the center of the river. Opening and closing, it makes a loud clacking sound as it prepares to feast. The creature's glowing red eyes are visible below the surface of the muddy river. The Kraken holds several other souls overhead like grapes about to be devoured. It begins releasing its victims who plummet into its mouth. As soon as it releases a shade, its tentacles plunge beneath the water searching for fresh souls to devour. Finally, it finally drops Marcus, who screams as he falls into the mouth of his tormenter.

Cælius has seen enough, he ducks behind the obsidian spire. There he hides, on the banks of the River Styx. He is out of breath and the vile water drips from his head and body forming a puddle around him. He is naked, alone, fearful, and full of regret. Whispering to himself, "What do I do? I drowned in sin before I could be saved by the Messias." Courage comes to him. *I must resist the temptation to give up. I must evade these monsters as long as I can. Since the Messias has not yet come, there may still be a chance to be saved... even here.* He thinks.

He retreats from the water's edge and hides with his back to the rocks. Cælius looks skyward but there is no sky, nor star in the black, stale air to gain his bearings. He is trapped. Sounds of violence, carnage, wailing, and weeping ring out. Just then, a strange movement draws his gaze toward the waters at his feet, to the mire in front of where he sits.

Cælius leans over, straining to investigate the water in the dim light. Something swirls in the mud and river foam. It moves like a snake. He spots a small tentacle, then more appear. He scuffles back to the rocky bank as the tentacles creep up on the obsidian stone toward him. The monster to whom they belong slowly rises out of the murky water.

It appears to be a twisted, more diabolical, siren of legend. A woman's naked torso, but with the hips and legs of an octopus. She is brownish-green in color, which makes her almost unnoticeable in the water. Her matted, bladderwrack seaweed hair covers her scaly, green shoulders and breasts. Oversized black eyes, like that of a shark, lock onto Cælius; she peers at him with a predator's gaze. Her slimy tentacles slip up and around his legs, there is no escaping her grip.

Raising her arm, she points a long boney finger toward him. "You cannot hide from usss, Cæliusss." She says with a gurgling hiss. The foul creature opens wide the gaping maw on her long face, exposing her rotten teeth. A narrow, forked serpent's tongue swishes about as she begins to sing her sinister and painful song.

Contrary to earthly sirens, she is not seducing Cælius, instead, she calls out to dæmons patrolling the shores. She bids them come and take him. Cælius closes his eyes, covers his ears, and screams out, "Deus meus, salva mea!"

Ioannes stares upward into the darkness from his knees. He searches for an answer to his condition, wondering when, or if, the remnant of hope he holds onto might give out. Without any explanation, his body freezes in this upward-looking position. A vision of events unfolding on the Earth above fills his mind and he forgets his place. Instead of a hellscape, he sees a garden at night.

The moonlight casts shadows in the light mist dancing through a grove of gnarled olive trees. A man kneels alone among the trees. He prays to Adonai, whom he calls "Father." He prays with his entire being, blood mingles with sweat from his brow. The man is in agony. Ioannes hears his words, "O, my Father, if it is possible, let this cup pass from me; nevertheless, not as I will, but as you will."

The vision fades to another image of the man standing in the garden, surrounded by others. A squad of Iudæus soldiers approach, led by a man who is not a soldier; he is dressed like the others. This man, leading the soldiers, greets the man in the garden with a kiss on the cheek. Again, Ioannes hears the man, "Judas, you betray the Son of Man with a kiss?" The Son of Man is immediately arrested and beaten while the rest of his friends fly into the night. This vision fades to another.

This Son of Man is chained and bound; he has been assaulted. He stands before a court of Iudæus Pharisees and is surrounded by many people making false accusations. Ioannes can see them gesturing and speaking but what they say is inaudible. The Son of Man remains steadfastly silent. The high priest steps forward and says something, but Ioannes cannot hear his words. Only the answer of the Son of Man reaches him. He says calmly and with authority, "You have said so. But I say to all of you: From now on you will see the Son of Man sitting at the right hand of the Mighty One and coming on the clouds of heaven." The chief priest tears his robes and wails at this response. The other priests spit on the Son of Man, while some strike him and mock him before taking him away. Then blackness.

Ioannes intuitively recognizes the setting of the next vision, it is the Antonia Fortress next to the temple mount. Light from the early morning sun illuminates the room in which the Son of

Man now stands. He is alone with a Roman Governor, who questions and studies him. Again, the Son of Man remains steadfastly silent until he gives a last response, "You say rightly that I am a king. For this cause, I was born, and for this cause, I have come into the world, that I should bear witness to the truth. Everyone who is of the truth hears my voice." Ioannes' heart begins to beat rapidly. Hearing only the Son of Man's voice in these visions, he begins to think he is witnessing the Messias himself. He watches the Roman Governor send him away. His vision blurs again.

The Iudæus King, Herod, who commissioned Cæsarea Maritima, strolls into his palace court. By the color of the light, Ioannes knows it is still morning. The Son of Man is led by chains to the court of the king, who is initially excited to meet him. The king fervently questions him and makes a request of him. Here the Son of Man says nothing, he does not speak a word. As a result, the king and his court mock him before sending him away.

The vision fades back to the Roman court. The governor makes a declaration. Soldiers seize the Son of Man and the vision fades.

Ioannes is released from his paralyzed state. He drops his head into his hands. Shame overwhelms him, whispering to himself. "Deus meus, what are you showing me? Is this Son of Man on whom all my hopes are pinned? Is he the Messias?"

He hears the scourging in the background. Ioannes covers his face with his shackled hands, flinching with each crack of the whip and each strike upon the Son of Man. He becomes aware that he is not the only one to see these visions either. Each time Jesus is marked with the whip, each time he is struck, dæmons and evil souls scattered throughout the darkness cheer. The roar is loud, as though it comes from a packed coliseum. Ioannes looks up again, his face a messy mix of tears and ash. He thinks to himself, *Again, I see the innocent man suffer, scourged, and beaten. Who is this man, that he would endure such abuse for those he called friends, brothers, and sisters? Who is he that dæmons would cheer so at his torture?*

A clear vision comes back. It is mid-day. A small dishonorable group of a garrison of soldiers hides the Son of Man away in an anti-chamber somewhere in Antonia Fortress after the scourging. He sits shaking in a corner, trying to suppress the pain of his beating. The legionnaires are supposed to be preparing him for Pilate, instead, they ridicule him. They smack his face and pluck hair from his beard. They wrap a scarlet cloak around him and brutally fix a crown woven from thorns upon his head. They mock him by bowing to him. They spit at him and call him names, all of which are inaudible.

Somewhere in the volcanic darkness of limbo a lesser dæmon squeals with giddiness, "Now these are my kind of soldiers!"

Ioannes hears this and, searching the dark landscape, exclaims in defiance, "How much more can this Son of Man, take? He has done nothing to deserve this!" He looks up again to see the Roman governor, standing with the Son of Man on the outer steps of Antonia Fortress. He has already offered a choice to the crowd. They have rejected the Son of Man and the governor released a criminal, who is seen entering the crowd.

The governor grows uneasy with the mob after their accusations and, half leaning toward the Son of Man, quietly questions him one last time. Ioannes still cannot hear what is shouted by the crowd or inquired of by the governor. The Son of Man, shaking from pain, looks the Roman in the eye to tell him, "You could have no power at all against me unless it had been given you from above. Therefore, the one who delivered me to you has the greater sin."

In the darkness of limbo, a chant begins to grow. Dæmons and condemned souls alike add their voices to the mantra of the earthly crowd, "Crucify him! Crucify him! Crucify him!"

Ioannes leans his head down and moves to cover his ears, but a sudden hush falls over Limbo. The only sound is the lava churning in the cauldrons. He doesn't know what has happened. Curiously, and cautiously, he looks up.

In the distant area, just over the black pit, the vast chasm, hanging in midair by his throat, is the traitor Judas. It is clear he had despaired and hung himself. Now he hangs from the very noose placed around his neck with his own two hands. All eyes watch the soul of this traitor descend into hell. With an eerie, flame-colored light on him, the hanged man slowly sinks through the dusky, ash-filled air, toward the distant pit.

Chatter, hisses, and noise increase as the traitor descends, climaxing when he nears the threshold of the abyss. There both dæmons and sinners curse him and hurl stones at him. They scream, "Traitor! Liar! You will suffer!"

Judas cannot wail or scream because of the noose tied around his throat but he does gnash his teeth and flail about wildly as he tries to defend himself from the stones. However, he promptly slips into the depths of the chasm near the lake of fire and is out of sight. Just as quickly as it started, the scene ends.

Then a different shout from somewhere in the black hellscape, "Guilty! Guilty!" A raucous cheer goes up, as though some gladiator had won a great victory. Jesus has been condemned and sent to be crucified.

Ioannes watches the Son of Man bear a heavy cross down the crowded Via Dolorosa in Hierosolyma. He can tell the burden is tremendous and witnesses him stumbling and dropping his cross. He falls atop it in exhaustion. He struggles to return to his feet. Some out of hate and others out of adoration, call out his name, Jesus. Soldiers continue to scream at him and whip him until he reaches locus Calvariæ[15]. There Jesus falls to the ground with his cross. He is stripped of his garments and then dragged on his back to place him on the cross, which is lying flat on the ground.

A legionnaire carpenter advances with hammer and nails in hand. He kneels next to Jesus' hand, which is already stretched out and tied by his wrists. The carpenter holds a nail to Jesus' palm with his left and raises his hammer with his right.

Ioannes cannot bear to watch any longer. He falls prostrate on the hot, black rock, burying his face in his hands. He knows what comes next. He weeps as he talks to himself, "This innocent man, the Son of Man, has already endured much. Whipped, beaten, and suffered more than I. He was led out to his death as I have been led here. He is nearly as naked as I am too."

The ping of hammer on nail resonates through the bare landscape of hell, echoing off the volcanic terrain and inciting dæmons to a disgusting ecstatic cry. They shout in frenzy

---

[15] Place of the Skulls – (translated from Latin (AKA Golgotha)

with each hammer blow, while Ioannes utterly sobs with each one. He shouts uncontrollably, "No, stop this! He does not deserve this!"

A lesser dæmon rushes out of the black wasteland and kicks Ioannes in the ribs, knocking the wind out of him and rolling him onto his side. The fiend stands over him, exclaiming in his bloodlust, "Shut up sinner!

The hammer strikes another nail while the dæmon strolls confidently back in the direction he came from, disappearing in the darkness. Ioannes reaches for his side. The pain in his ribs is nearly unbearable.

The hammering is done. Everything is relatively still in Limbo. Ioannes labors to catch his breath in the silence. He lifts his tear-stained face in time to see Jesus being raised on his cross.

Racked with pain, he hangs in the hot sun. He is flanked by criminals on their own crosses. To his surprise, Ioannes hears the taunts of the first criminal, "If you are the Christ, save yourself and us!"

As well as the retort of the second criminal, "Do you not even fear God, seeing you are under the same condemnation? We receive the due reward of our deeds, but this Man has done nothing wrong." Then, with great humility, the second criminal pleads to Jesus, "Lord... remember me when you come into your kingdom."

"Amen..." His voice is broken. "I say to you, today..." He labors ", you will be with me in Paradise."

Ioannes witnesses the mercy of Jesus. His lamentation stops; a flicker of hope appears in his weary eye. Short of breath, he whispers to himself, "Truly, he must be the Messias." He continues to watch the unfolding scene on earth with great anticipation.

Still hanging from the cross, Jesus is broken, exhausted, and at his end. He looks skyward and exclaims, "Father, into Your hands I commit my spirit!"

Those in the first circle of hell watch as Jesus breathes his last, dying on the cross. A raucous cheer erupts, as loud as 20 filled coliseums. In the distance, a lesser dæmon shouts with joy, "What a glorious day in hell!"

Ioannes merely falls prostrate in sorrow. However, the merriment of the damned rapidly

subsides. All fall silent and still; a great hush
blankets the underworld.

Chapter 11: The Appearance

The Siren's song has stopped. She no longer twists her tentacles around Cælius. Things have gone eerily silent. The strange moment causes him to open his eyes in a squint and slowly pull his hands away from his ears.

Though still in her slimy clutches, the Siren pays no attention to him. She is distracted by something happening downriver, some unknown place beyond the fog. He slowly turns his head to see what she is looking at. It is then he notices two winged dæmons out of the corner of his eye. They are standing just above and behind him on the higher part of the riverbank.

Similar to the goblin-like dæmons but a little bigger and browner in color, they too have stopped in their advance and are staring downriver. Something is not only causing a great hush to descend upon the river but is also making every hellish creature stop in its tracks. Even the waves have begun to flatten. There is an odd feeling in the air, as though there has been a collective deep breath before they plunge beneath the waves.

* * * * *

Ioannes rises painfully to his knees trying to see what is happening around him. The sound has been completely sucked out of the air; it is an eerie and uneasy calm until... 'KRA-BOOM!' A deafening thunderclap shakes the ground. It startles Ioannes, who instinctively reaches to cover his ears and duck his head. The sound wave reverberates through his chest before rumbling across the muffled black sky, breaking the uncomfortable silence.

After it passes, he returns his gaze skyward. There, just above the volcanic maelstrom in the blackest sky is a point of pure, twinkling white light. It burns brighter than any star in the earthly night sky; brighter than any flash of lightning or burning ember in the hellish atmosphere. It begins to expand into the shape of a giant round orb.

At first, the yellow-white orb appears like the sun as seen through an ash cloud of an erupting volcano. Unlike the sun, it is encircled by a spinning band of golden fire, sparking as it spins around the orb. This flickering band releases a great wind that blows the ashen clouds away in all directions.

Then, in the bright circle of white light, a figure appears, the silhouette of a man. He seems both far away and near at the same time. He stands upright with his hands extended slightly outward from his sides. Though it is hard for Ioannes to distinguish the figure's details, his appearance throws all of hell into a panic. Throughout the darkness, sounds of fearful scurrying like a field of rats trying to hide from a great, golden hawk. The skin of any demon unfortunate enough to have the pure light land upon him, burns. They scatter and run seeking shelter among any shadow they can find.

* * * * *

Cælius, who was already looking downstream, curious as to what captivates the attention of the winged dæmons and the siren, hears the same massive thunderclap. Though it is farther away, it is still more powerful than the ones in the tempest that sunk his ship. It rumbles across the pitch sky and echoes along the rocky banks. He sees the same, single point of pure light, which twinkles before expanding out into the shape of a giant orb. The same great wind blows upstream, dispersing both smoke and fog on the River Styx.

Though he is far from it, Cælius can still see the shape of a man in the light of the orb. He was not blessed with visions of the Passion of the Christ, yet his soldier's intuition tells him this can only be one thing, the arrival of the Messias. Cælius knows only he could appear in this way. He becomes visibly excited, like a child who sees his father returning home after a long journey.

Sounds of chaos near the light itself spread outwardly in all directions. The appearance of the figure in the light has indeed plunged the denizens of hell into widespread panic.

* * * * *

Evermore shadows are displaced by light. A new dawn rises over the desolate hellscape. Ioannes watches as the unseen becomes visible; volcanoes, lava flows, and even the distant pit can now be seen with more clarity. This new dawn is not welcome by all, however.

Out of the chasm a deep roar erupts in opposition to the light. It shakes the landscape in view, including the very ground Ioannes is chained to. Rocks tumble and shake as the ground quakes. A deafening voice, filled with rage, defiance, and contempt yells out, "No, Son of the Most High, these souls are mine! I will not part with a single one!"

All sound, even the echo from the voice of the devil himself, is quickly muted as Jesus begins to speak. Though none can see him speak, the sound of his voice is heard by all. It is soft but strong, comforting but with authority. His speech is in perfect cadence and pronunciation. "Silence. You will have only what my father wills you to have. I am here for the just who went to sleep before I had come. I am their shepherd, and they will know my voice, for I am the way, the truth, and the life."

Ioannes, who is already on his knees, notices the unnamed soul, and all of Limbo by the sound of it, bending a knee to the Messias. All is silenced as Jesus commanded.

The shape of the orb begins to change. From it, light stretches out above, below, and to the left and right forming the shape of a cross. The overall effect of the beams of light resembles what will one day be known as a monstrance, with Jesus at its center.

With a great explosion, the most brilliant white light, gold around its fringes, bursts forth from the orb. The gold fringe appears to shimmer, sparkle, and crackle before expanding outward and descending all around. Ioannes quickly realizes it is not a normal, shimmering light, but that each light is itself alive. Angels, each one invading the underworld. They are sent out to find the just who await salvation.

As the holy legion descends in all directions, Ioannes notices the figure in the orb growing in stature. Though his silhouette is still dark, light shines through holes in his hands and feet.

* * * * *

The Siren unconsciously relaxes her grip. Cælius is on his knees along with the dæmons behind him. He sees the angels descending. He watches in desperation, hoping they will come to the River Styx. Unfortunately, they do not appear to be doing so. He grows desperate. Wrestling completely free of the stunned Siren, he jumps to his feet, and, waving his hands, shouts like a castaway sighting a ship nearby, "Elohim! I am here! I am here! Do not forsake me, Lord. Please!"

His screams shake his would-be captors from their confusion. The first shore dæmon jumps down the bank and strikes him in the back of the head with a cudgel. It knocks him down, belly first, on the smooth stone between the Siren and the sharp spires. He falls on one of her tentacled arms too, both hurting and insulting her.

Enraged, she quickly winds all her large tentacles around his torso securing his arms. She wraps a smaller one around his neck and squeezes his throat. She brings her horrid face close to his, which is turning red from strangulation. She gives him a malevolent smile before she reaches around his shoulders and places her jagged fingernails near his spine. She then drags them outwardly to his shoulders, tearing his flesh while laughing with delight. "You hurt me, I hurt you."

Cælius winces in agony. She leans back toward the river, loosening her grip. His arms are now free and he falls to the ground gasping for breath. He looks up at the wicked siren. She licks at the blood on her fingertips with a morbid pleasure before gurgling a hiss of contempt, "Now, get off me sssinner!"

The dæmons, standing between Cælius and the bank, watch her assault with satisfaction. Placing his palms on the ground shoulder length apart. With searing pain, he weakly lifts himself. The Siren pulls her slimy tentacle out from under him.

He lets himself down and reaches to wipe the muddy water from his face. Before he can though, the dæmons waylay him. The first one grabs him by the hair on his head and pulls him back up to his knees. Standing behind, knee in Cælius' back, he bends down to chortle a growling whisper in his ear, "They're not coming for you. You, shade, are not even in hell yet!"

He flings Cælius back down on the rock. Like the blackness of the water that took his life, despair consumes him. He feels as though he has been cast off on a small island somewhere near Greece and must watch his ship, captain, and crew abandons him. He feels bewildered and lost.

The first dæmon keeps his knee in Cælius' back while the other dæmon grabs his hands, bringing them behind his back. This time he does not resist. He only wonders if his past sins were too great to be forgiven. He doubts his worthiness to be rescued by the Messias. *He will not come for me; I am lost. Adonai has judged me unfit for salvation and sentenced me to hell to be forever tormented.*

* * * * *

Closer to Ioannes, the silhouette, still illuminated by the sun-like orb, continues to grow in size. It becomes easier to see the figure. It **is** Jesus the crucified who stands in the light. The look on Ioannes' face changes from awe and curiosity to surprise and uneasiness. He unknowingly murmurs to himself, "Wait, is he coming toward me? How can this be? Surely, I am not worthy of the Messias, the Son of the living God. What do I do?"

Awestruck, Ioannes watches Jesus' approach for a moment longer. The Messias is clothed in the purest white linen, and he walks on a billowing white cloud, which gracefully descends toward him.

Ioannes is visibly nervous; lightly shaking with trepidation. His heart pounds faster with both fear and hope. Sitting on his feet, he bows his head low, almost to his knees, again murmuring to himself, "Might I be blessed by he who conquers death?"

Though he is on his knees, the unnamed soul holds his head up high in arrogance and pride. He leans toward Ioannes slightly, whispering in a low voice, "Shut up stultus and listen to me! Don't you recognize the adversary? This is an elaborate trick to lull you in. He is Lucifer, the Morningstar, don't be tricked by his light or his appearance. Our time has come. He is here to take us deeper into the pit, to greater punishment. Don't trust him!" The shade straightens himself back up in defiance.

Ioannes keeps his head bowed, but his eyes open. There are no footsteps, as Jesus sets no foot in that forsaken place, yet the light around him gets much brighter. He knows the Messias draws near. In a voice as firm and soft as a devoted father speaking with love to his young child, Jesus calls his name, "Ioannes."

Ioannes shutters. It is impossible to keep the tears of joy from running down his cheeks at the sound of the Messias' pure voice. Yet, still hiding his face in his ash-covered hands, he responds with fear and humility, "I am here Lord." He removes his hands from his face and clasps them together tightly at his chest. Through a parched throat and split lips, he continues, "Domine miserere nobis[16]. Please, Lord, have mercy on me."

Ioannes' heart thumps against his chest. His body, still racked with pain, aches with the rush of blood pulsating through it. Tears stream uncontrollably from the young man's eyes making his face a black, muddy mess. He finds it hard to breathe and sob at the same time. His body trembles.

Jesus squats down to meet him. He reaches out and places his hand gently, yet firmly, on Ioannes' shoulder. In that instant, everything changes. The prostrate soldier is calm and unafraid. He no longer trembles; he is still. He takes a deep breath and, based on his previous visions of the passion, focuses on the image of Jesus' face in his mind.

The Messias speaks to him. "My child. I know you. I have seen all you have done in the

---

[16] "Lord have mercy" – (translated from Latin)

belief of my Father, the one true God. Though they were slaves, you gave food and clothing to the ones who taught you my father's commandments. From then on, I watched you seek out the truth; although you may not have known it was me you sought, me you fed, me you clothed, and me you served.

You were gifted with the vision of my passion and my sacrifice. You cried out for me and now, I am here for you. Will you trust in me? Will my grace be enough for you? Do you accept the gift of salvation I offer?"

Ioannes answers without hesitation, "My Lord, though I feel I have been no servant of yours, and therefore am not worthy of you, yes, still, I trust in you with all my heart. The grace you offer is more than enough for me. Truly, you are the Messias, the Son of God, and I humbly receive you."

With his head still down, Ioannes does not see the joyful smile on Jesus' face. The Lord draws a slow, steady breath and exhales upon the humble soldier. His exhale moves through Ioannes' hair and down his back, blowing soot and ash from his body. The shackles click open and fall from his wrists, which are still clasped together at his chest. His burns, wounds, and bruises disappear; his skin is cleansed and made whole.

Immediately following this, he hears the rush of enormous wings. One from the legion of angels hovers just above and to Ioannes' left shoulder. His wings beat rhythmically, making a whoosh sound with each flap. Jesus removes his hand from Ioannes and stands. Wind from the angel's wings blows away the ash and filth from all around them. Then the angel lands on the ground next to Ioannes, his sandaled feet lighting quietly on the ground. He folds and tucks his translucent wings behind him.

The angel appears as a perfect copy of a man in his early 30s, but somehow more elegant; his skin radiates holy light. He has no discernable race; he appears to be mixed between Africanus, Asian, and Caucasian. He bows to Jesus, upon arrival.

The angel wears a deep blue, leather breastplate, trimmed in gold. His armor is set against a light gray tunic with a golden belt wrapping his waist. A golden scabbard holds an ivory-handled gladius at his side. His sandals are the same golden color as his belt and the trim on his armor. He holds something made of cloth in his hands, which he transfers to his belt behind his back.

He reaches down, takes Ioannes' hand, and lifts him to his feet. He is several inches taller, so they are not quite face-to-face. The angel pulls the cloth from the belt behind his back and unfolds it. He swiftly clothes Ioannes with a pale blue, linen robe, and then wraps a golden sash around his waist. Once he is done, he smiles at Ioannes before slightly dipping his head and motioning with his left hand toward Jesus.

Ioannes turns reverently toward his savior who, standing on a cloud, is slightly elevated and looking down on him with unfathomable love. His eyes blaze forth in a deep copper color, as though they were made of the molten metal. Divine light emanates from his face; from his entire being. An overwhelming sense of undeniable joy fills Ioannes' heart and soul and a wide smile spreads across his face.

The Lord says, "The faith and hope you clung to has saved you Ioannes." He takes a step closer, continuing, "I still have much to accomplish here and in the world above. Go now to paradise. Great joy awaits you there." Jesus pats him on the shoulder and offers an encouraging smile, "We will be in my Father's house very soon; after I have fully accomplished my father's work. For now, you must go further up and further into my kingdom."

Jesus turns to move throughout the forsaken precipice to the abyss, claiming others as he claimed Ioannes, who lingers with the angel for a moment. Together they watch evil souls and dæmons alike flee as the Magnificent One brings ever-expanding light to Limbo and joy to those who awaited his coming.

The angel presently turns to Ioannes, officially introducing himself, "I am Præsidiel. Come, my friend, as our Lord said, it is time to leave this forsaken place."

He stretches out his white, translucent wings, which reflect God's holy light. He gestures to rise, and then places his arm around Ioannes' back, beneath his shoulders. The two begin to ascend toward the perfect orb of light still spiraling in the black sky.

Ioannes observes thousands of similar angels rising into the light with them, each accompanying another soul. In the darkness of hell, they first appeared as glinting points of light but, as they all move closer to the orb, their glory is truly visible. "See, our Lord comes for his servants and prophets of old, as well as others who believe in him and followed the commands of Elohim. He is the good shepherd who seeks out his lost sheep." Informs Præsidiel.

Ioannes has no words, he quietly smiles. He thinks back to the moment Jesus died on the cross; how the dæmons cheered as if it were a great victory for them. It was not that moment, no. It is this moment, the moment of the Messias' appearance in hell, the salvation of those God still loves and had not forgotten, and the ascension of the just into His kingdom, **this** moment is what made it a **truly** glorious day in hell.

The chasm between the threshold of light and Limbo increases exponentially. Ioannes' vision remains locked on the oscillating orb of light, his emotions swelling with youthful anticipation of the world to come. Quickly forgotten and fading rapidly in the distance is the hellscape from whence he came, where another shade is being taken in the opposite direction.

There, a horrible, twisted creature clutches the ankle of the hate-filled, unnamed soul. It drags him across the jagged landscape toward the edge of the black pit. His wrists are still bound in irons and being drug on his belly, the soul's outstretched hands reach out beyond his head. His fingers rake through loose gravel and rocks, desperately trying to grasp onto something, anything that might pause his unwilling journey downward. The pompous demon who fancied himself a judge follows at his side, antagonizing him, kicking him, and spitting on him. He delights in the soul knowing he is bound for darkness and fire.

The two men, once bound in a field of black pumice, have finally departed for their eternal destinations. One is taken to paradise; the other is left to his destruction. Ioannes has already forgotten most of his earthly life, rather he is enthralled by the prospect of Elysium. Unnamed Soul, however, will be forever reminded of his sins and is repulsed by his prospects. Ioannes blinks as he passes through the gateway into blinding white light.

* * * * *

Cælius lies on his belly, hands bound behind his back. He shakes his head trying to get the filthy water from his face. He looks up to his right where the hideous face of the Siren glares back at him, a disturbing smile upon her wretched face. The two dæmons are standing between him and the rocky bank behind them. The first one says, "Pick him up. Since he's already on this side of the river, we'll just take him straight to the judge."

The second shore dæmon grasps Cælius by the right arm and yanks him up. Once he is on his feet, the other demon grabs his left arm. Together they drag him up the bank to higher ground. The fallen warrior finally gets a clear view down the River Styx. However, in the distance, there is an unexpected sight. The Messias is coming toward them.

Jesus walks just above the surface of the now calm water, the small cloud under his feet keeps him from touching its filth. His light illuminates the river valley as he walks with a steady pace, full of purpose. He is already ahead of the raider ships and striding directly toward them. The dæmons see the Son of God too. They drop their prisoner at the sight of him and scurry off. The Siren gasps turns and plunges back into the mire.

Cælius, stunned, watches in awe from his knees as Jesus approaches. However, he suddenly becomes conscious of all his sins. Out of fear and shame, he does something foolish, so very 'uncharacteristic' of a well-disciplined soldier. Hands still tied securely behind his back, he quickly, and clumsily, stumbles back down the bank to the rock on which he crawled out of the river on. He kneels behind the spires and hides in his shame.

Cælius begins muttering to himself, "My sins, I never completed the purification ritual. Murder, lust, selfish pride, more than that... How foolish am I to think I could ever be worthy of the Messias? How foolish am I to think salvation would come to me on the banks of the River Styx? Think! What am I to say? What am I to do?"

Wisps of cloud move around the spire and fill the area around him. He falls prostrate, knowing Jesus has come.

He hears his name, "Cælius." Calls the Messias.

A shiver runs down his spine. It is the same voice he heard the day he buried his friend Ioannes. His nose stings as he tries to hold back the tears welling up in his eyes. He is desperate to control his emotions. Though he still hides his face in shame, he responds faithfully, "I... I am here my Lord."

"Why do you hide from me?"

"I saw you coming and was fearful. I am a great sinner Lord, and I am ashamed." He pauses briefly, slightly lifts his head, but not high enough to look at Jesus, and then boldly says, "I saw your angels descend into the underworld, but not here. I thought... I thought, surely, I was lost... condemned."

Jesus stands in front and to the left of Cælius. Just as he did with Ioannes, the Messias squats down in front of the former soldier and sailor. With the greatest of compassion, he reaches down and places a hand under Cælius' chin and gently lifts his face so they might see each other. "Peace to you Cælius."

Cælius looks up into his molten copper eyes. His smooth bronze skin radiates the purest light, and his dark hair and thick beard are clean and oiled. His features are soft, yet firm. Jesus looks upon him with such profound love, as a father does for his child. A peacefulness enters the heart of Cælius as Jesus releases his chin and begins to speak to him. "Did you not call to me?" Cælius answers with his longing eyes. The Savior continues, "You are right to admit your sins. However, you were not in the world when I taught. If you were, you might understand that my love, my mercy, is not something to be earned through the completion of any ritual. True salvation is a gift, a gift to those who believe in me. Baptism is an outward sign offered by those who accept my gift."

He pauses for a moment. Cælius knows he cannot hide his thoughts from the Son of God, yet a visible love and mercy are shining forth from the Messias' face as he speaks. "I taught this lesson to those who could hear, let me also ask you. Suppose a shepherd has a hundred sheep and loses one of them. Does he not leave the ninety-nine in the open country and go after the lost sheep until he finds it? And when he finds it, does he not joyfully put it on his shoulders and return home?" He pauses briefly to let the questions sink in. "Do you understand this parable Cælius?

"Yes, Lord, I think, I hope, I understand. *You* are the good shepherd and I hope... beyond all hope... that maybe I am the lost one you seek."

Jesus chuckles with delight and stands up. Cælius remains on his knees but sits up on his legs listening to the great teacher. "Amen, I say to you, I love your unshakeable hope, your optimism. I have seen your works, Cælius, both good and evil. I know the sins of your youth, your sins as a soldier, and your sins as a sailor. However, I also know you repented and amended your life when you began to seek out my Father, the one, true and living God. Your optimistic will to continuously ask, seek, and knock in search of the truth has always pleased me." He offers a smile.

"I also know you willingly laid down your life for your shipmates. There is no greater love than that, to lay down your life so that others may live. I too, laid down my life so that others may live eternally. I paid the price for all sin, and I have the power to forgive those who trust in me. So, Cælius, do you believe that I have the power to do this? Will you accept the gift I offer?"

Cælius looks deeply into the eyes of Christ, knowing full well who he is. Desperately trying to restrain the tears in his own eyes, he lifts himself to one knee, hands still tied behind his back, and confesses, "Truly, you are the Messias. I am sorry for my sins with all my heart. If you are willing to forgive, my Lord, then yes, I gladly trust in you. Your grace, your mercy, is enough for me."

Jesus smiles. "Your sins are forgiven Cælius, your faith has saved you." At the very sound of Jesus' words, Cælius' bonds are instantly loosed. All the water, mud, and filth fall from his body. Even the wounds on his back are healed. His strength is regained. He, like Ioannes, is set free, cleansed, and made whole.

Still on bended knee, but now with hands freed, Cælius rubs his wrists. He then bows his head and strikes his breast with his right hand, offering Jesus a soldier's salute. After this, he looks up at him again. Jesus smiles and motions with his right hand to look downriver. Coming quickly toward them out of the distant, volcanic wasteland is a brilliant angel, one of the hosts who held open the orb of light.

His enormous translucent wings beat harmoniously, moving him swiftly through the dark sky. He swoops slightly upward at the edge of the water on the other side of the spires. The wind from his wings blows gently on them as he lands on the high bank. He bows to Jesus and then extends his hand down to Cælius. They clasp forearms and the Angel lifts him up the rocky bank. He then reaches behind his back and pulls out a pale blue robe. He helps cloth Cælius with it and then ties a golden sash around his waist. He smiles and places a hand on Cælius' shoulder. "There. That is better."

Jesus rises up the bank on the cloud. Cælius turns to face him. Jesus smiles. "I am pleased you called to me Cælius; however, I still have much to accomplish here, and in the world above. It is time for you to enter paradise now. There you will find great joy and we will meet again, very soon; after I have fully accomplished my father's work."

Cælius slightly bows his head and lightly strikes his breast in salute once more. Jesus turns back toward the forsaken, hellish landscape from which he had originally appeared. Again, his stride is swift and purposeful as he departs them.

Cælius turns to face the Angel, who says, "Come. As the Lord commanded, let us leave this cursed shore for the white shores of Elysium." Without haste, he stretches out his white, lustrous wings. He places his right arm under Cælius' left arm, wraps it around his upper back, and gestures upward. They began to ascend swiftly toward the orb of light in the distance.

Cælius disregards his former surroundings as they fly above the River Styx. Dæmons still scurry about its banks, hiding from the light of Christ. Frightened souls willingly crawl aboard the ships of the damned, bound for hell. Even the tentacles of the unseen monster plunge back below the blood-stained waters.

As the Angel climbs toward the orb, the distant landscape of hell comes into sight, but Cælius pays it no mind. Charon's ferry is seen pushing ashore and beyond that, what looks like a desolate, volcanic wasteland. Cælius, his eyes fixated on the light, sees none of it. The great chasm opens between hell and the gateway. All the features of the underworld are engulfed by the empty, black void. The angel says with a smile as they prepare to pass into the blinding white light, "Hold on."

Chapter 12: A Discovery in Heaven

Everything on the other side of the orb is much brighter and more vivid. All the colors seem far more brilliant. An angel carries a man with his arm around his back. They light on a soft, verdant, grassy outcropping. The angel folds his wings, and then speaks, "Welcome to Paradise Ioannes."

"Thank you, my friend." Ioannes closes his eyes and lifts his face to the sky, soaking in its warmth. He re-opens them, slowly surveying the lush, sprawling domain. He takes a deep breath and exhales, continually marveling at the landscape. Fields of tall grasses, meadows filled with many kinds of colorful flowers, and deep green forests with a variety of flowering and fruit-bearing trees. Wide, rolling hills surround the meadows and forests. Streams of the clearest water flow down from vast, snowcapped mountains rising behind the rolling hills, and wind in various directions.

A fresh, cool breeze ruffles his robe, and Præsidiel's wings, as it carries floral scents throughout the wide lands of Heaven. "Even the fabled Elysian Fields cannot compare to this." Acknowledges Ioannes. Præsidiel laughs.

Ioannes thinks as he observes, *All of creation has not only been remade but is laid out before me. I find the prospect of finding and knowing my savior in this place all the more than exhilarating.*

In the distance, a great, gleaming city sits majestically upon a hill. It is how he always envisioned the picturesque Jerusalem. Its tan and white stone buildings beckon new arrivals to enter through its wide gates and wander its sacred streets. In the sky above it, millions of stars, and even other worlds are visible. The sky itself fades from a bright blue to twilight, and on to starlit heavens beyond the luminous city. From the city flows a pure river, clear as crystal. Just below the city, a massive tree straddles the river. Ioannes can make out twelve different fruits in its lush canopy, one of which appears to flash with lightning trapped inside.

He observes in his mind, *here there will be no more darkness, no more weeping and gnashing of teeth, no more war, no death or despair. I see only life, love, truth, and joyous discovery laid out before me, just as he promised.*

Ioannes turns to Præsidiel, who can easily read the unbridled joy and curiosity on his face.

The angel smiles, tilts his head in a slight bow, and motions with his left hand toward the road leading up to the city on the hill. Ioannes feels like a child being released into an ethereal playground. Ioannes nods back in gratitude, while lightly striking his breast in salute. He takes his first step into the Kingdom of Heaven.

He begins up the road toward the city, reflecting as he walks, *some might call those of us redeemed from the precipice of hell the 'just pagans' of the world... Me? I am simply happy to have been called by our Lord at all. Truly, I am content in having all of eternity to express my gratitude, to express my eternal thanks for the sacrifice, the mercy, and the grace of our Lord Jesus, the Christ.*

* * * * *

Ioannes walks with a slow, steady, joyful, and observant look in his eye. He follows the well-laid, stone road toward the gleaming city on the hill. The road is perfectly hewn out of the hills, rising toward the city. It is lined by outcroppings of rock with small grasses and blue squill flowers popping up between the rock. Small fig trees and patches of purple lavender also adorn the road. Beyond it, on the right side, lay beautiful fields of green wheat. A light and fragrant breeze moves across its surface and the grass sways and moves with it like waves on the water.

Further up, on the left side of the road, a rather lush olive tree has grown up between tan boulders. Though Ioannes continues to observe his newfound surroundings, as well as smile and greet others moving up the road with jubilation, he keeps his focus on the olive tree. As he grows closer, the true detail and beauty of the tree stand out. Its massive, brown trunk twists and turns upward as though it has been dancing and twirling in the presence of Elohim for thousands of years. Ripe green olives fill its leafy canopy.

Ioannes approaches to touch its trunk and, out of the corner of his eye, notices a subtle, less traveled trail, branching off from the road. His curiosity is peaked. He stops, climbs up on one of the boulders near the tree, and rests for a moment. He observes the path and its destination from the elevated position. It runs almost parallel, albeit much more winding, toward the city on the hill, meandering between the main road and a pure stream. A long row of enormous eucalyptus trees lines a portion of the winding path ahead. Beyond that, a short waterfall cascades over a small rock face, not far from where the brook branches off from the river of life flowing from the city. The sparkling clear waters splash beautifully on the tan rocks below.

Both the trail and the stream call to him; inviting him to follow it onward and upward. He wonders aloud as he looks around, "Surely, I am not the only one to notice this path?" Many other men, women, and children, from every race and culture, even some he has never seen before, move with much excitement up the road toward the city. All languages are easily understood by each person in heaven, and he cheerfully waves and greets a family (a father, mother, and two young daughters) as they pass by his lofty perch upon the rock.

Another man approaches. One dressed in a way Ioannes has never seen. Ioannes observes him closely. The Chief wears light tan pants made from animal skin; leather-like tassels running down the sides of each leg. He has on a long sleeve cloth shirt, blue in color, over which is an ornate breastplate of sorts made from two columns of tiny bones. Feathers tied to the ends of leather tassels adorn the bottom of it, as well as a silver disc in the middle. For all his ornamental dress, the Chief wears no shoes or sandals.

On his head is an opulent headdress. The blue band with orange designs woven into it stretches across his forehead. On each side are decorated, red discs from which two white feathers hang. Rising from the top of the band and encircling his head like a halo is 30 to 40 feathers. Each one is white with a black tip. The shaft of each feather is wrapped in tan leather and red string and fixed to the thick blue headband.

Long, jet black, and braided hair, protrudes down from under the feathered headdress and rests on each of his shoulders. His dark brown facial features are rugged, and he has a solid, warrior's build. His stride is proud and happy, yet purposeful as if he were seeking the soul of another who would be there. The Chief raises his hand when he greets Ioannes, saying with a smile, "Háu kola."

Ioannes immediately understands it to mean "Hello friend." He returns the greeting in kind, "Salutate amicus."

Still sitting upon the boulder, he curiously watches the Chief pass by, saying to himself, "What an interesting man. I hope to meet him again."

Returning to his previous thoughts, he turns his eyes skyward where, in the clear deep blue sky, angels of all types are seen flying to and fro. Some with a human form, some made of pure light, some with six wings, and some with less. He looks back down at the rock upon which he sits and, for a fleeting moment, has a single thought, a regret, which he expresses softly, "I wish I would have told so many more about the Messias, especially my friend Cælius. I pray God might save him from the fires of hell too."

A warm, scented breeze rustles the olive leaves, and the thought vanishes as quickly as it had come. The wind blows toward the side path, directing his attention there. The sound of the babbling stream reaches his ears. Like a siren, it calls again to him. Without hesitation, and with confidence Ioannes slaps his thighs and declares, "It is decided then, I will follow the path less trodden."

He hops down, places his feet on the new path, and with the enthusiasm of a young boy, sets off on the trail.

Having walked a good distance up the new path, Ioannes nears the eucalyptus trees he saw from the boulder. There the trail comes close to the stream, so he stops to kneel at a little sandy bank. He dips his hands in the cool, clear water. A rainbow trout darts upstream and draws his eye further up the trail where he notices the first, large eucalyptus tree to the right side of the trail.

A man is sitting on a grassy outcropping between the trail and the tree. He is leaning against the trunk of the fragrant tree. The man's gaze is fixated on the water flowing in the stream. Ioannes whispers to himself, "There is something familiar about that man; the way he stares at the water. I know I have seen that look before."

He stands and continues up the path to greet the man. To his great surprise and delight, he realizes the man is a friend and fellow legionnaire. Truly excited, he quickens his pace.

Nearly running, he shouts and waves, "Cælius! Cælius, my friend!"

Shaken from his contemplative stare, Cælius turns to see Ioannes rushing toward him. He jumps to his feet, and, raising his arms, exclaims, "Salve, frater meus!¹⁷"

Ioannes runs off the path and up the grassy outcropping with hands outstretched. They meet with a brotherly hug, patting each other on the back, and then pull away to take a good look at each other. Cælius keeps his hands on the younger Ioannes' shoulders, who is filled with excitement at finding him. Ioannes says, "I worried I would never see you again, my friend."

"Oh, but I had a feeling I would see *you* again, brother."

Still stunned to find his friend and mentor, Ioannes babbles with a youthful exuberance, "I... I don't know what to say. I am overjoyed to see you." A curious look suddenly comes over his face. "Forgive me, but how did you come to this place?"

"Ha, ha, ha. Calm yourself, little brother. I am here because of you. If not for you, I may

---

¹⁷ "Hello, my brother!" (translated from Latin).

never have learned about our Lord Jesus, the Messias."

"Indeed! Were you saved by him too!?" It dawns on Ioannes what he has just asked. "What am I saying? Of course, you must have been. He is the way!"

"Yes, my friend, he is the way, the truth, and the life. I do not have the words to express just how grateful I am for his mercy."

Cælius releases Ioannes but they continue to stand, conversing, on the grassy outcropping under the faint shade of the eucalyptus tree.

"Truly. As am I." begins Ioannes. "Of all the ways leading to the city on the hill though, I find you here."

"An angel brought me to the trailhead by the olive tree. He suggested I follow the path along the stream, and so I did." Cælius states. "Well, until I came to this beautiful eucalyptus tree. Here, the beauty of this place interrupted my thoughts. I have seen so many shorelines and waters since you and I last spoke. I sailed the deep blue waters of the Mare Internum and swam in the blood-stained, muddy waters of the River Styx."

Ioannes interrupts, "Wait, you were in hell too?"

"No. No, I never made it that far. Our Lord saved me while I was stranded on the river's bank. The horrible things I saw there before he came…" Cælius' voice trails off as though he is already forgetting his time in the underworld. "Anyway, that is why I stopped here. I have never seen such crystal-clear water as this. I was drawn to its purity. I took a refreshing sip and then rested for a moment. Here I sat, contemplating the unfathomable mercy and love of our savior, Jesus. I was thinking of words to express my gratitude and love. Out of the hundreds, no thousands, of souls I saw in the underworld, how he could be so gracious to save one such as me…" His voice trails off a bit. "After all, I have seen, I was content to rest peacefully under the tree, in the presence of Elohim." Cælius slaps Ioannes on the shoulder and grins. "Until I heard your voice that is. A very pleasant surprise indeed! Now I am here with you, my brother, the one who started me on the path to God so long ago."

Before Ioannes can respond, the familiar sound of angel's wings beat overhead. Slowing his descent, the angel lands on the trail ahead of them. Both men exclaim simultaneously, "Præsidiel!" The two men turn to look at each other with joyful surprise. They realize at that moment that Præsidiel had served as each of their escorts into paradise.

Præsidiel folds his wings, raises his hand to greet the two men, and, approaching them with a grand smile, says, "Dominus vobiscum[18]!"

Ioannes and Cælius, being former soldiers, strike their breasts and bow their heads in salute, saying in unison, "Et cum spiritu tuo[19]."

Then, without hesitation, each man takes a turn clasping Præsidiel's forearm and shaking their new friend's hand. The angel asks, "What a glorious little spot, yes? I thought this would be a wonderful place for you two to reunite. Ioannes, I knew you wouldn't resist the adventure of the side trail." Præsidiel winks at him in jest. "Have you had a moment to share your stories; to share the glory of our Lord Jesus' saving grace?"

"I had only just begun. I have not yet heard Ioannes' tale. Join us?" Asks Cælius.

---

[18] "The Lord be with you!" (translated from Latin).
[19] "And also with you!" (translated from Latin).

"Unfortunately, no. I came to retrieve you, my friends. Our Lord's work is nearly complete. He will be returning soon. All the heavenly hosts are preparing for his coronation." Præsidiel motions for them to accompany him as he starts up the trail toward New Jerusalem. "Come. Come, you can recount your tales on the way. We can relive the love and mercy of our magnificent creator as we go to his feast. Time to go further up and further into His glorious kingdom." The two former soldiers follow happily.

* * * * *

Upon reaching the city on the hill, Præsidiel gives Ioannes and Cælius light blue tunics with white, linen togas to wear, which is more suitable attire for the upcoming coronation and feast. He then escorts them both into an indescribably lavish, Romanesque banquet hall.

Elaborate tapestries hang from high walls, supported by massive, ornate pillars. High, vaulted ceilings are covered with frescos honoring the Holy Trinity. Many tables fill the hall. Some are short, Middle Eastern tables, while others are long, European-style tables. A magnificent bounty fills each one. Some souls recline at table, others sit in tall chairs, while stIll more stand in joyful conversation. The blending of peoples and cultures from all over the world is striking, to say the least. The great hall is filled with gleeful chatter praising God in the highest.

Angels escort souls to the hall and help them find a place at the table for the celebratory feast. Præsidiel shows Ioannes and Cælius to seats at a long, low table. Both men look around at others coming to sit. One such soul is the Chief Ioannes met at the crossroads. He carries his headdress under his arm at his side. Ioannes jumps up to meet him, "Hello again my friend. Please, excuse my earlier manners, I am Ioannes. I was hoping we might meet again."

The Chief smiles, but before they can have a conversation, a loud click is heard, the latch of a large door. Every angel, every soul, grows silent. Those who were reclining or sitting now stand. All eyes turn their attention to the two enormous, opulent, marble doors at the end of the room as they begin to swing open. The purest bright light shines through the gap, filling the room with God's holy light. The silhouette of Jesus appears in the light. He raises his hands and the light shines through the holes in them. He declares, "Welcome good and faithful servants! Welcome to the joy of your Father's house!"

THE END

"Hope is the pillar that holds up
the world. Hope is the dream of
a waking man."
~ Gaius Plinius Secundus
(aka Pliny the Elder)

About the Author

John Eudy is a twenty-six-year military veteran. He was both a soldier in the Army National Guard and a sailor in the U.S. Coast Guard. Having lived in ten different towns and cities in five states, and having visited forty other states and territories, including Guam, he is well-traveled. He retired from military service in 2015.

After spending three short years working in the civilian sector, John officially retired to pursue his dream of becoming a published author. Inspired by faith and scripture, he enjoys weaving history, cultural legends, life experiences, and Christian morality into fictional tales.

John and his family currently reside in their native Missouri. He has been married to his lovely wife of nearly thirty years, and they are the proud parents of four daughters, two of whom are already with God in heaven.

Made in the USA
Columbia, SC
22 November 2022

71582453R00085